Discarded from
Garfield County Public
Library System

Garfield County Libraries
Carbondale Branch Library
320 Sopris Avenue
Carbondale, CO 81623
(970) 963-2889 • Fax (970) 963-8573
www.GCPLD.org

MELISSA DE LA CRUZ

Blue Bloods

THE GRAPHIC NOVEL

ADAPTED BY
ROBERT VENDITTI

ART BY
ALINA URUSOV

COVER ART BY
FIONA STAPLES

LETTERING BY
CHRIS DICKEY

HYPERION
New York

Adapted from the novel *Blue Bloods*

Text copyright © 2013 by Melissa de la Cruz
Illustrations copyright © 2013 Disney Enterprises, Inc.
All interior artwork by Alina Urusov, with special thanks
to Jimmy Xu, Jennifer Munro, Jin Laxus Forge, Ramon
Amancio, and Scott Forbes

All rights reserved. Published by Hyperion, an imprint of
Disney Book Group. No part of this book may be reproduced
or transmitted in any form or by any means, electronic or
mechanical, including photocopying, recording, or by any
information storage and retrieval system, without written
permission from the publisher. For information address
Hyperion, 114 Fifth Avenue, New York, New York 10011-5690.

Design by Jim Titus

Printed in the United States of America
First Edition
10 9 8 7 6 5 4 3 2 1
V381-8386-5-12306
Library of Congress Cataloging-in-Publication Data
    Blue Bloods: the graphic novel / by Melissa de la Cruz ;
adapted by Robert Venditti ; art by Alina Urusov. -- 1st ed.
    p. cm.
    Summary: Select teenagers from some of New York
City's wealthiest and most socially prominent families learn
a startling secret about their bloodlines.
    ISBN 978-1-4231-3446-6 (hardback)
    ISBN 978-1-4231-3447-3 (paperback)
1. Graphic novels. [1. Graphic novels. 2. Vampires—Fiction.
3. Wealth—Fiction. 4. Secrets—Fiction. 5. New York (N.Y.)—
Fiction.] I. Urusov, Alina, ill. II. De la Cruz, Melissa, 1971–
Blue bloods. III. Title.
    PZ7.7.V48Blu 2013
    741.5'973—dc23   2011053237

Visit www.bluebloodsbooks.com
and www.un-requiredreading.com

SUSTAINABLE FORESTRY INITIATIVE
Certified Chain of Custody
At Least 20% Certified Forest Conte
www.sfiprogram.org
SFI-00993

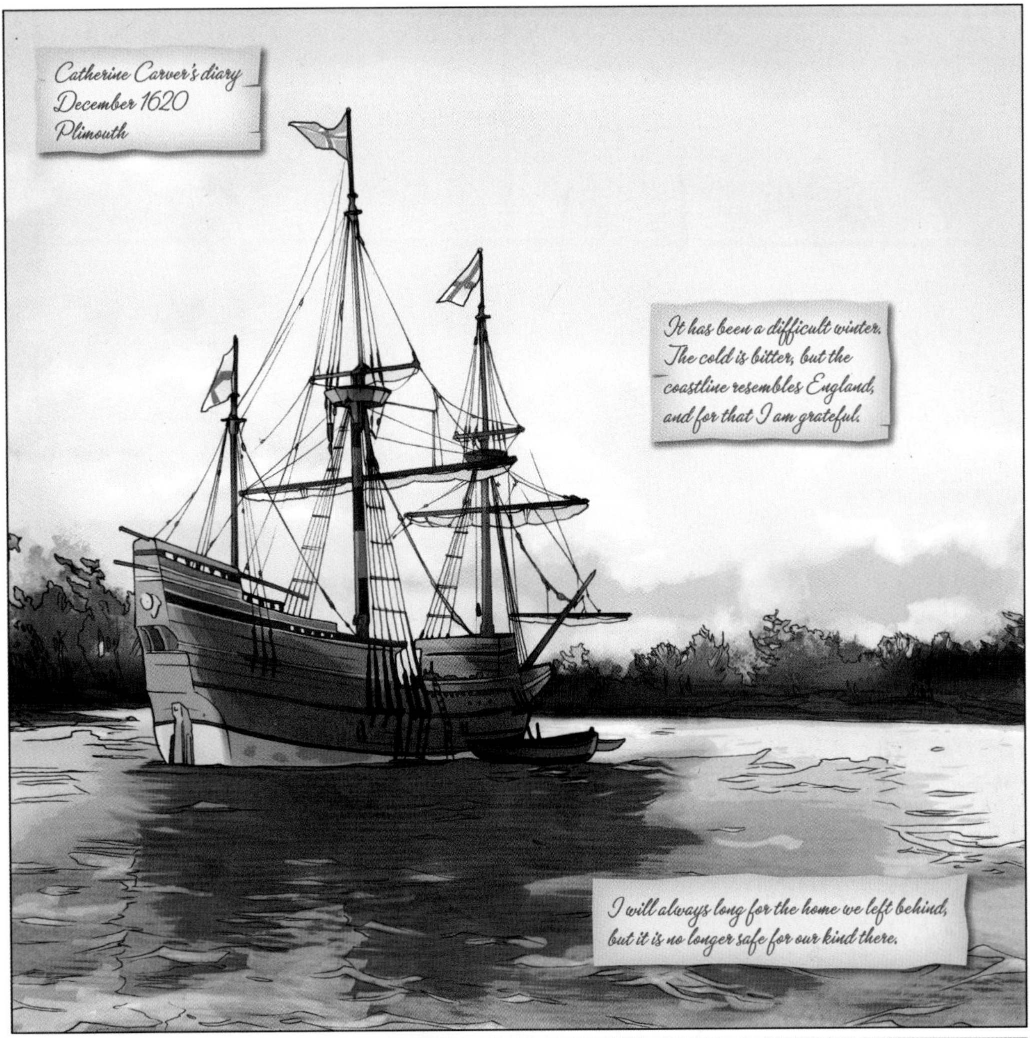
Catherine Carver's diary
December 1620
Plimouth
It has been a difficult winter. The cold is bitter, but the coastline resembles England, and for that I am grateful.
I will always long for the home we left behind, but it is no longer safe for our kind there.

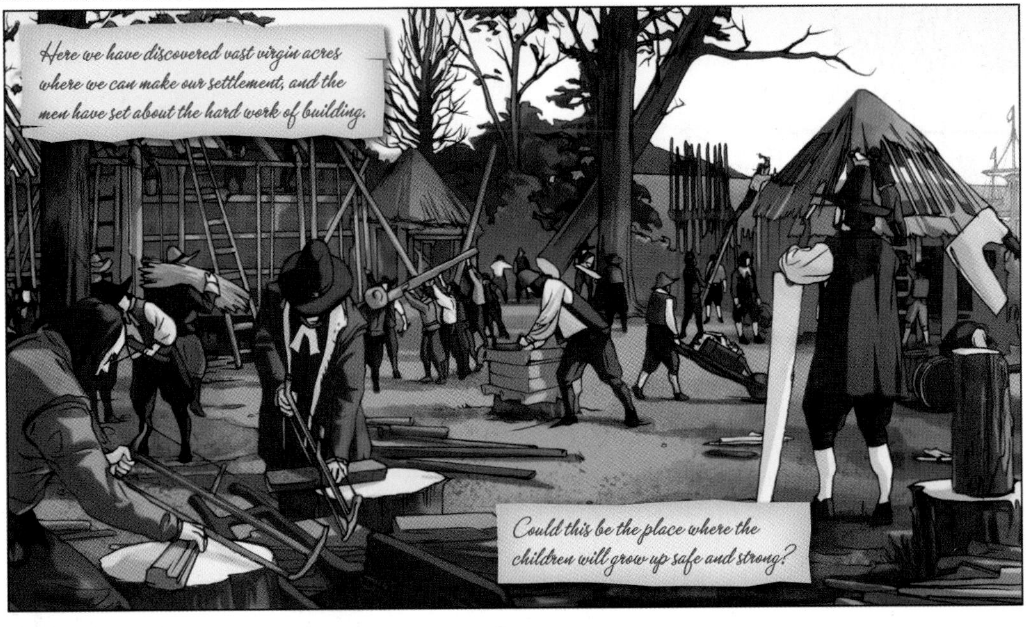
Here we have discovered vast virgin acres where we can make our settlement, and the men have set about the hard work of building.
Could this be the place where the children will grow up safe and strong?

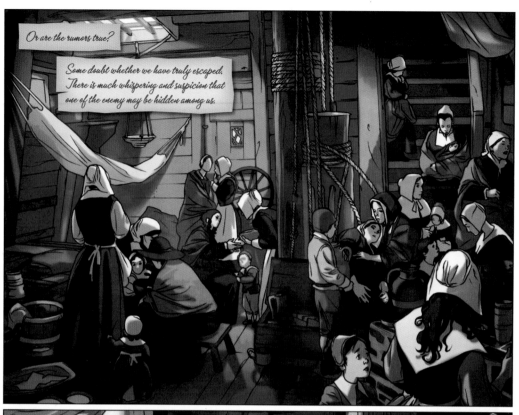

Or are the rumors true?

Some doubt whether we have truly escaped. There is much whispering and suspicion that one of the enemy may be hidden among us.

And now the Billington boy has gone missing.

Taken, some say.

For a time I comforted myself with the knowledge that I have not felt or seen anything, that my visions would warn me if the danger was real.

No longer.

When we first spied our leader, Myles Standish, returning with his group from their trip to resupply Roanoke colony, we were overjoyed.

Indeed, news that our sister settlement to the South was faring well would buoy the hopes for our own new venture.

But alas! Standish brings word that Roanoke is disappeared. The men found no shelters, no animals, nor any of our kindred.

Nothing remains of Roanoke except a bare patch of field.

That, and a tree carved with a single, terrible word:

We are cursed!

The enemy is here.

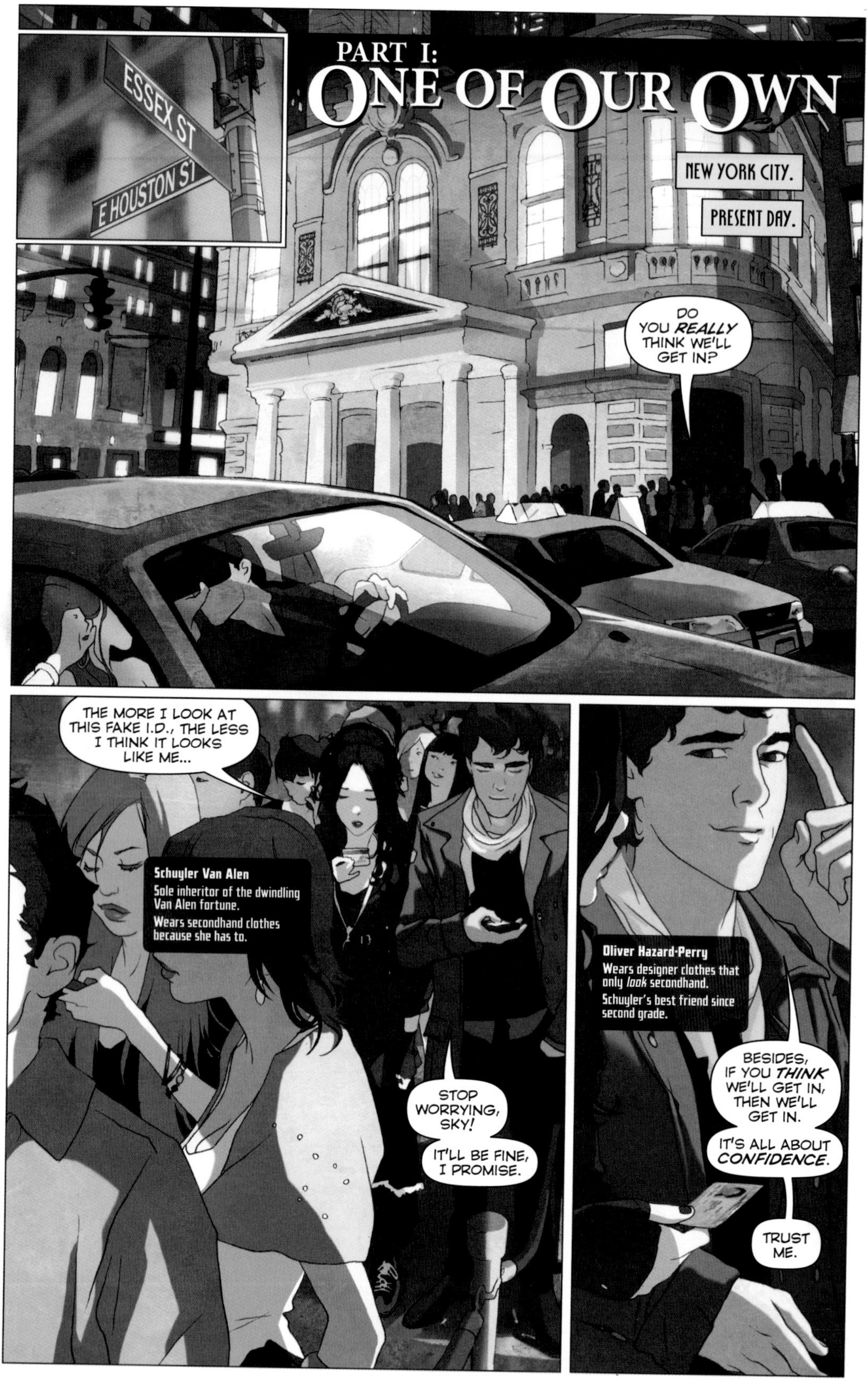

ESSEX ST
E HOUSTON ST
PART I:
ONE OF OUR OWN
NEW YORK CITY.
PRESENT DAY.
DO YOU REALLY THINK WE'LL GET IN?
THE MORE I LOOK AT THIS FAKE I.D., THE LESS I THINK IT LOOKS LIKE ME...
Schuyler Van Alen
Sole inheritor of the dwindling Van Alen fortune.
Wears secondhand clothes because she has to.
STOP WORRYING, SKY!
IT'LL BE FINE, I PROMISE.
Oliver Hazard-Perry
Wears designer clothes that only look secondhand.
Schuyler's best friend since second grade.
BESIDES, IF YOU THINK WE'LL GET IN, THEN WE'LL GET IN.
IT'S ALL ABOUT CONFIDENCE.
TRUST ME.

WHERE DOES HE THINK *HE'S* GOING?

Jack Force. **THE** Jack Force. You'll see.

EVENING, JACK.

RIGHT THIS WAY.

Told you.

OLLIE! *WHAT* ARE YOU DOING?

FOLLOW HIM! GO!

I.D.'S, PLEASE.

NATURALLY.

REMEMBER, THINK *POSITIVE*.

WAIT. THIS ISN'T RIGHT...

LET US IN. LET US IN.

JUST *LET US IN!*

...

ENJOY YOUR EVENING.

WHAT'D I TELL YOU? NOW, LET'S HAVE SOME *FUN*.

GEE, *GOOD TIMES.*

LET ME GUESS: YOU'RE LOOKING FOR *JACK,* AREN'T YOU?

I'M JUST... CURIOUS.

RIGHT. WELL, IT'LL TAKE MORE THAN A *FAKE I.D.* TO GET WHERE HE IS.

WHY? WHERE IS HE?

WHERE ELSE?

"HE'S IN THE V.I.P. AREA, WHERE HE CAN LORD IT OVER EVERYBODY. BUT DON'T WORRY--

"--I BET IT'S BORING. NO OXYGEN, ANYWAY."

If Oliver only knew how right he was!

I'M SO BORED.

Mimi Force
Twin sister to Jack.
Undisputed queen bee of the Manhattan hive.

MAYBE YOUR DATE WOULD BE MORE ENTERTAINING IF YOU BOTHERED TO FOLLOW THE COMMITTEE'S RULES.

WHERE'S THE EXCITEMENT IN THAT?

ANYWAY, HOW COULD I RESIST?

HE'S SO... DELICIOUS.

YOU COULD STAND TO GET SOME YOURSELF, YOU KNOW. SO GRUMPY ALL THE TIME.

I'M GOING TO GET SOME AIR.

YOU. MAKE SOMETHING HAPPEN.

...uhnn...

LIGHTWEIGHT.

LEAVING ALREADY?

HEY, AGGIE.

I'VE HAD *ENOUGH* FOR ONE NIGHT.

YOU TWO BETTER GET BACK INSIDE, THOUGH. MY SISTER HATES NOT HAVING AN *AUDIENCE.*

HE'S RIGHT, YOU KNOW...

YOU GO ON AHEAD. I'LL BE THERE IN A MINUTE.

Bliss Llewellyn
Recently transplanted from the great state of Texas.
Cheerleader.
Senator's daughter.
Trying to fit in.

Augusta "Aggie" Carondolet
Mimi's wannabe.

SHOOT!

LOOKING FOR THIS?

Dylan Ward
New bad boy in town.
Tempting...

THANKS.

UM, I'M BLISS.

OF COURSE YOU ARE.

PLEASE TAKE YOUR SEATS, CLASS--

--I'M AFRAID I HAVE SOME *VERY SAD* NEWS TO SHARE THIS MORNING...

WE'VE JUST BEEN INFORMED THAT AUGUSTA CARONDOLET HAS *PASSED AWAY.*

APPARENTLY THERE WAS AN... INCIDENT AT A NIGHTCLUB THIS PAST WEEKEND, AND DOCTORS WERE UNABLE TO ATTEND TO HER IN TIME.

AS YOU ARE AWARE, AGGIE HAD BEEN A STUDENT HERE AT DUCHESNE SINCE *PRE-KINDERGARTEN.*

CLASSES HAVE BEEN SUSPENDED FOR THE REMAINDER OF THE DAY, AND THERE WILL BE A *FUNERAL SERVICE* TOMORROW MORNING BEFORE SCHOOL. YOUR ATTENDANCE IS *EXPECTED.*

THE THOUGHTS AND WELL-WISHES OF THE *ENTIRE* FACULTY GO OUT TO THE CARONDOLET FAMILY, AS I AM SURE DO YOURS AS WELL.

WOW, THAT'S *HEAVY*, MAN. I SAW HER AT THE CLUB ON FRIDAY.

I, UH, MET SOMEBODY.

THAT REMINDS ME...WE WERE SUPPOSED TO MEET UP WITH YOU. WHAT HAPPENED?

SHE JUST WENT OUT TO *MAKE A CALL*, AND THEN SHE DISAPPEARED. WE STILL DON'T KNOW WHAT HAPPENED...

SO *AWFUL!*

IS THERE *ANYTHING* YOU NEED US TO DO?

HEY--

--SORRY ABOUT YOUR FRIEND.

WHAT DO *YOU* KNOW ABOUT IT, *WASTOID*? YOU JUST MOVED HERE.

I'VE KNOWN HER *FOREVER*. SHE LENT ME HER FAVORITE JEANS ONCE, AND *NEVER EVEN ASKED FOR THEM BACK!*

THAT'S A *TRUE* FRIEND...

TOTALLY!

WHATEVER!

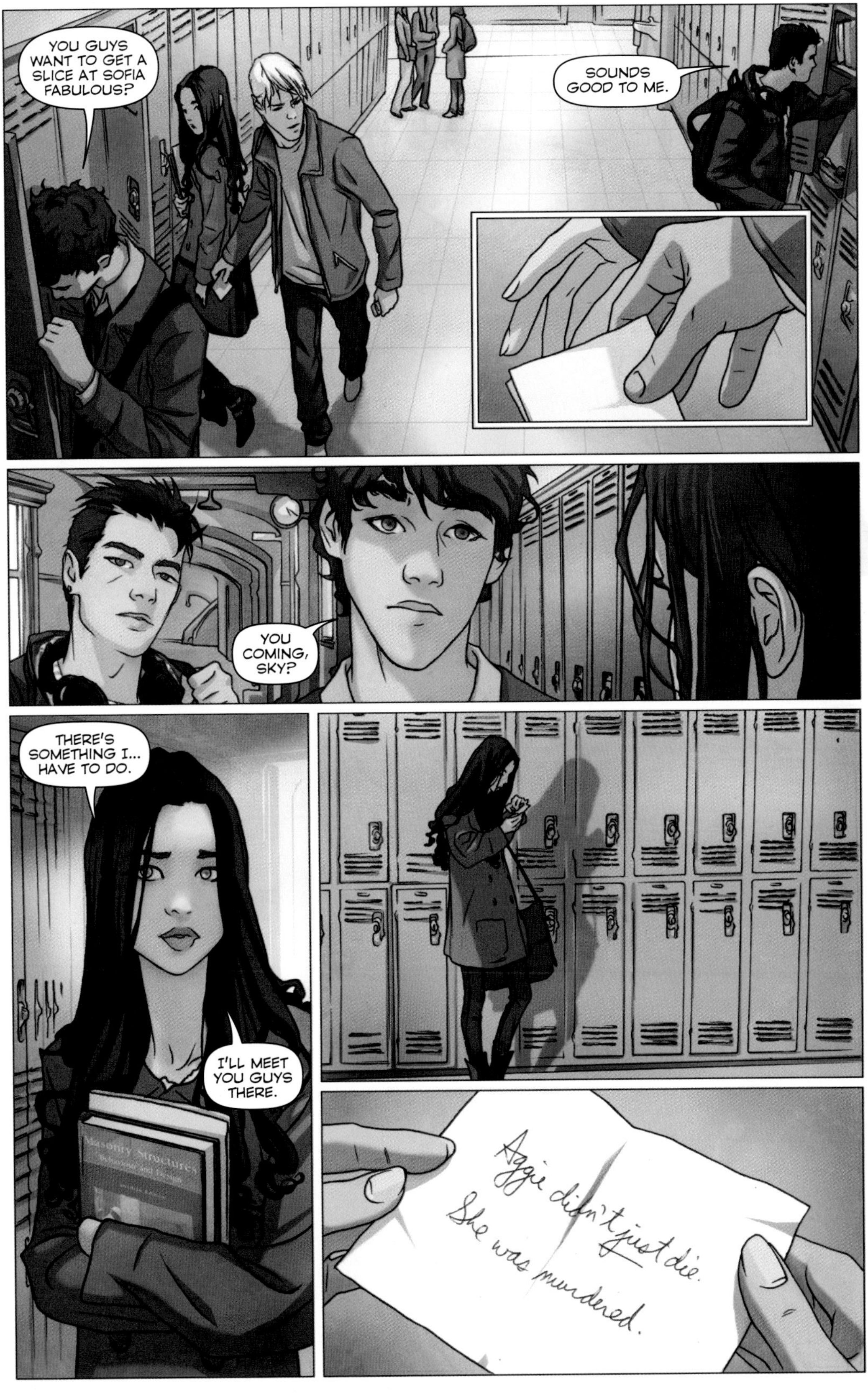
YOU GUYS WANT TO GET A SLICE AT SOFIA FABULOUS?
SOUNDS GOOD TO ME.
YOU COMING, SKY?
THERE'S SOMETHING I... HAVE TO DO.
I'LL MEET YOU GUYS THERE.
Masonry Structures
Behavior and Design
Aggie didn't just die.
She was murdered.

DARLINGS!

BobiAnne Llewellyn
Bliss's stepmother.
You know what they say: everything is bigger in Texas. Especially the diamonds.

I WAS SO *WORRIED!*

TAKE IT EASY, BOBIANNE. WE'RE FINE.

I *DO* WISH YOU'D CALL ME "MAMA," DARLIN'.

I WISH YOU'D STOP PICKING US UP IN THE *ROLLS-ROYCE* EVERY DAY...

EVEN THE FORCES TAKE CABS.

NOT THAT WE NEED *ANY* RIDE AT ALL.

I WON'T HEAR A WORD OF IT, NOT AFTER WHAT HAPPENED TO THAT CARONDOLET GIRL! HER MOTHER IS IN *SHOCK*, THE POOR THING.

YOU GIRLS ARE *NOT* TO GO OUT ANYMORE WITHOUT A CHAPERONE. YOU ESPECIALLY, BLISS. THERE WILL BE NO MORE SNEAKING OUT WITH MIMI TO *WHO KNOWS WHERE.*

YOU'RE TO BE HOME EVERY NIGHT BY NINE. YOUR FATHER *INSISTS.*

BEFORE I FORGET, THIS CAME FOR YOU TODAY.

"THE *NEW YORK BLOOD BANK COMMITTEE* CORDIALLY INVITES YOU TO JOIN ITS MISSION."

WHY WOULD I WANT TO JOIN SOME *SNOBBY CHARITY CLIQUE?*

YOU DON'T *JOIN.* YOU GET *CHOSEN.*

DO I *HAVE* TO?

I DIDN'T THINK THEY WERE INDUCTING NEW MEMBERS UNTIL NEXT SPRING.

BUT DARLING! IT'S THE MOST EXCLUSIVE CHARITY IN *ALL* OF NEW YORK.

ALL THE CHILDREN OF THE *RIGHT FAMILIES* ARE MEMBERS.

MIMI JOINED LAST YEAR. IT'LL BE GOOD FOR YOU, YOU'LL SEE.

AND IT WOULD MAKE *YOUR FATHER* AND ME VERY HAPPY.

WELL, IN *THAT* CASE...

WHERE WERE YOU ON FRIDAY NIGHT?

AT *THE BANK*. YOU KNOW, THE CLUB THAT WAS WRITTEN UP IN *US WEEKLY* LAST WEEK.

Jordan Llewellyn Bliss's half sister.

WHY, WHO WANTS TO KNOW?

THAT'S WHERE THAT GIRL GOT KILLED, ISN'T IT?

SO?

YOU KNOW WHO DID IT, DON'T YOU?

YOU WERE THERE.

ACTUALLY, I HAVE *NO IDEA* WHAT YOU'RE TALKING ABOUT.

IT WAS PROBABLY AN *OVERDOSE* OR SOMETHING.

NOW, GET INSIDE.

SORRY, HATTIE.
I FORGOT MY KEYS
AGAIN.

HEY, BEAUTY!

WOOF!

MISS ME, GIRL?

SLURP!

HOME SO SOON?

SCHOOL LET OUT EARLY. AGGIE CARONDOLET... DIED.

I KNOW. ARE YOU ALL RIGHT?

Cordelia Van Alen
Schuyler's maternal grandmother. Nothing **maternal** about her.

SURE.

WE WENT TO THE SAME SCHOOL, BUT I DIDN'T REALLY *KNOW* HER. SHE HUNG WITH A DIFFERENT CROWD.

HOW ARE YOUR ARMS?

THEY DON'T HURT OR ANYTHING. THEY JUST *ITCH* A LITTLE.

THE MARKS ARE BECOMING MORE PRONOUNCED. YOU MUSTN'T FORGET YOUR APPOINTMENT WITH DR. PAT.

ROWRR

OH, *DON'T WORRY* ABOUT ME, GIRL. I'M NOT GOING ANYWHERE.

I HAD A DOG LIKE THIS ONCE, WHEN I WAS YOUR AGE.

YOUR MOTHER DID AS WELL.

YOU'LL BE VISITING HER THIS SUNDAY, I ASSUME.

SAME AS *EVERY* SUNDAY, CORDELIA. I MAY NOT HAVE THAT MANY MEMORIES OF HER FROM BEFORE. BUT SHE *IS* MY MOTHER.

A FINE ONE SHE WOULD HAVE MADE, TOO, IF NOT FOR HER CONDITION.

WHICH IS MORE THAN I CAN SAY ABOUT YOUR FATHER.

WOULD YOU TELL ME ABOUT THEM? THERE'S SO LITTLE THAT I--

DINNER AT SIX, CHILD. *DO* WASH UP BEFOREHAND.

I NEARLY FORGOT: I WILL BE ATTENDING THE FUNERAL WITH YOU IN THE MORNING.

YOU MAY NOT HAVE BEEN CLOSE WITH AUGUSTA, BUT THE VAN ALENS AND THE CARONDOLETS HAVE A LONG *HISTORY* TOGETHER.

AND THERE WAS AN ENVELOPE FOR YOU IN TODAY'S POST. I LEFT IT ON YOUR PILLOW.

JUST A FEW MORE!

IT'S TIME WE WENT INSIDE. THE SERVICE IS BEGINNING.

OH... YEAH--

Charles Force
Father to Mimi and Jack.
The **real** power behind
New York City.

"--IT'S *AGGIE'S* DAY."

CHARLES. IT HAS BEEN TOO LONG.

HAS IT?

A *TERRIBLE LOSS*, YOUNG AUGUSTA. ALTHOUGH IT COULD HAVE BEEN PREVENTED.

YOU KNOW AS WELL AS I THAT THEY SHOULD HAVE BEEN *WARNED* ABOUT--

ENOUGH. NOT HERE.

ALWAYS THE FIRST TO SHY AWAY FROM THE TRUTH. YOU ARE THE WAY YOU HAVE ALWAYS BEEN: *ARROGANT* AND *BLIND.*

IF THE *CONCLAVE* HAD LISTENED TO ME, THE ENEMY WOULD NOT BE ON THE *HUNT* ONCE MORE. WE WOULD NOT BE HERE TO BURY *ONE OF OUR OWN.*

IF WE HAD LISTENED TO YOU AND *SOWN THE FEAR,* WE WOULD ALL BE *COWERING* IN CAVES.

YOU *MUST* RAISE THE ALARM! WE MAY STILL *STOP THEM,* IF YOU WOULD ONLY FIND IT IN YOUR HEART TO FORGIVE.

ALLEGRA...

DO NOT SPEAK TO ME OF ALLEGRA. I WOULD *NEVER* HEAR HER NAME SPOKEN TO ME AGAIN.

GOOD DAY.

‡pfft‡ WHO WEARS *WHITE* TO A FUNERAL?

YOU KNOW MR. FORCE? AND HOW DOES *HE* KNOW MOM?

COME ALONG, CHILD.

SCHUYLER! WAIT!

WHY DID YOU IGNORE MY NOTE?

I...UH... THOUGHT IT WAS A PRANK.

A *PRANK?* YOU THINK AGGIE'S DEATH IS *FUNNY?*

I DON'T EVEN *KNOW* YOU!

WE'VE HAD CLASSES TOGETHER ALL OF OUR LIVES, AND YOU'VE NEVER EVEN *GLANCED* AT ME.

NOW, ALL OF THE SUDDEN, YOU'RE PASSING ME NOTES ABOUT *MURDER?* WHAT AM I SUPPOSED TO THINK?

I...

I SAID *COME ALONG,* CHILD.

"YES, CORDELIA."

YOU GOING IN, OR NOT?

OH... UM... HEY.

...ARE YOU?

NAH. I THINK AGGIE WOULD BE MORE OFFENDED BY MY PRESENCE THAN IF I DIDN'T GO AT ALL. I KNOW *MIMI* WOULD.

I *SHOULD* GO.

BUT THE IDEA OF SITTING JUST A FEW FEET AWAY FROM A DEAD *BODY*...

WANNA CUT?

WHAT?

YOU KNOW, CUT. DITCH. *SKIP IT.*

WHAT BETTER WAY TO HONOR SOMEONE'S LIFE THAN TO GO ON LIVING YOUR OWN?

YEAH. I THINK I'D LIKE THAT.

THE METROPOLITAN MUSEUM OF ART.

I'VE BEEN MEANING TO COME HERE EVER SINCE I MOVED TO THE CITY.

I *FIGURED* THERE WAS A SOUL UNDERNEATH THOSE POM-POMS.

NOW, CLOSE YOUR EYES. I HAVE A SURPRISE.

WHAT?

JUST *DO* IT.

⹁giggle⹁

WHERE ARE YOU TAKING ME?

TRUST ME.

READY?

YES!

LOOK.

WHOA.

I KNOW. CAN YOU IMAGINE WHAT IT TOOK TO BRING AN *EGYPTIAN TEMPLE* ALL THE WAY TO A MANHATTAN MUSEUM?

IT'S SO... *BREATHTAKING.*

YEAH, *SHE* IS.

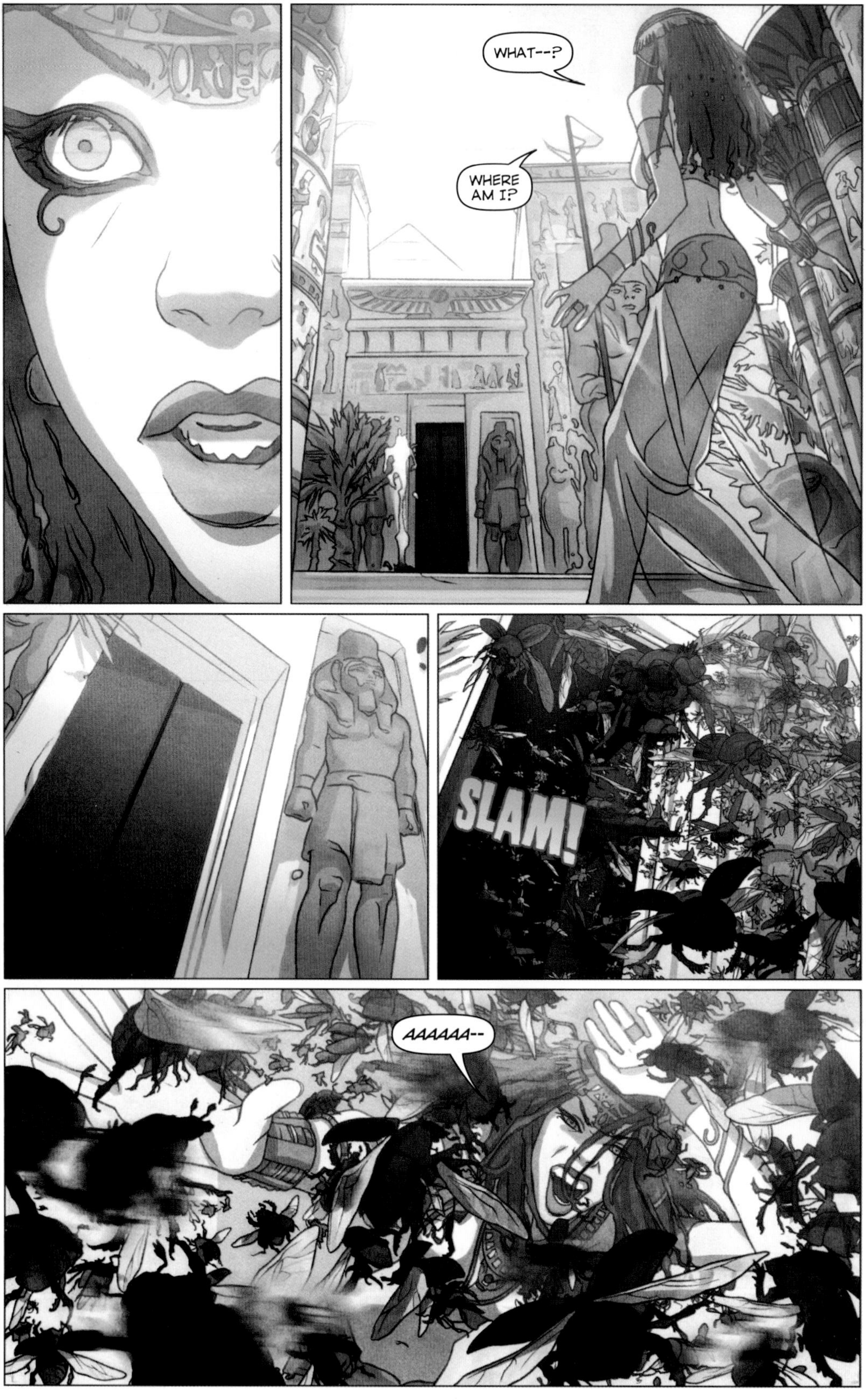
WHAT--?
WHERE AM I?
SLAM!
AAAAAA--

--AAAAA!

BLISS! WHAT'S THE MATTER?

WHERE ARE WE? WE WERE AT THE MET--THE EGYPTIAN EXHIBIT--AND THEN...

IT WAS LIKE I *TRAVELED BACK IN TIME* OR SOMETHING.

RIGHT...

IS ACTING *PSYCHO* YOUR WAY OF TELLING ME YOU'D RATHER GO TO A FUNERAL THAN HANG OUT WITH ME?

WHAT? NO!

I MEAN, I'M JUST MESSING WITH YOU.

GOTCHA!

GOOD. BECAUSE I'D *REALLY* LIKE TO SEE YOU AGAIN.

PART II:
BEAUTIFUL MONSTERS

BELLISSIMA.

TRY READING THE SIGN ON THE DOOR NEXT TIME. THE *MEN'S* DRESSING ROOM IS DOWN THE HALL.

I SAW YOU IN THE STORE. WHAT COULD I DO, BUT FOLLOW?

REALLY, I'M IN A HURRY. AND IT'S ALREADY BEEN A DIFFICULT MORNING.

PERHAPS YOU NEED SOMEONE TO CHEER YOU UP.

THERE ARE *RULES* AGAINST YOU BEING BACK HERE.

RULES? THERE ARE NO RULES WHEN IT COMES TO SOMEONE OF SUCH *BEAUTY*.

OH, YOU HAVE *NO* IDEA.

TEN MINUTES LATER...

KNOCK KNOCK

MISS FORCE?

I'VE SELECTED A FEW OF THE LATEST ARRIVALS FOR YOU TO TRY ON.

I'LL TAKE THEM ALL. BOX THEM UP AND HAVE THEM SENT OVER.

I'M LATE FOR A *BIG DAY* AT SCHOOL.

SHALL I BOX UP THE SUIT YOU ARRIVED IN AS WELL?

KEEP IT. MAYBE YOU'LL GET LUCKY, AND SOMEONE YOU KNOW WILL *CROAK.*

¿groant

...uhnn...

WELCOME TO
DUCHESNE CAREER FAIR!

FARNSWORTH
MODELING AGENCY

VERY GOOD. THANK YOU.

WALK'S A LITTLE ROUGH, BUT VERY TEACHABLE.

YES, WE *MUST* HAVE YOU AT FARNSWORTH.

REALLY?

THAT'S ALL FOR THIS VISIT, STUDENTS. WE'LL SEE YOU AGAIN NEXT SEMESTER.

KEEP PRACTICING AND MAYBE *YOU* WILL BE FARNSWORTH MATERIAL.

WAIT! THERE'S STILL ONE LAST AUDITION.

HMM...YES. YOUR PROPORTIONS ARE *IDEAL*, MY DEAR.

BUT HOW'S YOUR WALK? A *FABULOUS WALK* IS WHAT IT'S ALL ABOUT, YOU KNOW.

WELCOME TO ... ONE CAREER FAIR!

OH, *INDEED!*

STOMP!

STOMP!

STOMP!

TELL ME, WOULD YOU LIKE TO BE A *FARNSWORTH GIRL*?

GLAMOROUS PHOTO SHOOTS! TRAVEL TO EXOTIC LOCALES! PARTIES!

OF COURSE! I'VE ALWAYS THOUGHT THAT I WAS *PROFESSIONALLY* BEAUTIFUL.

LIKE A YOUNG KATE MOSS!

NO! DO YOU REALLY THINK--?

NOT YOU. *HER.*

WHO MIGHT *YOU* BE, MY DEAR?

SCHUYLER VAN ALEN?

I SEE YOU'VE DONE YOUR HOMEWORK. A MODEL SHOULD ALWAYS DRESS AS *PLAINLY* AS POSSIBLE FOR HER GO-SEES.

I DON'T--

CLICK

MAY I TAKE A POLAROID?

WRITE YOUR NUMBER HERE.

WHEN WE FIND A DESIGNER WHO WANTS TO USE YOU, WE'LL CALL.

OKAY...

HER? A *MODEL*?

SHHH.

CONGRATS. I GOT PICKED, TOO.

THANKS... I GUESS.

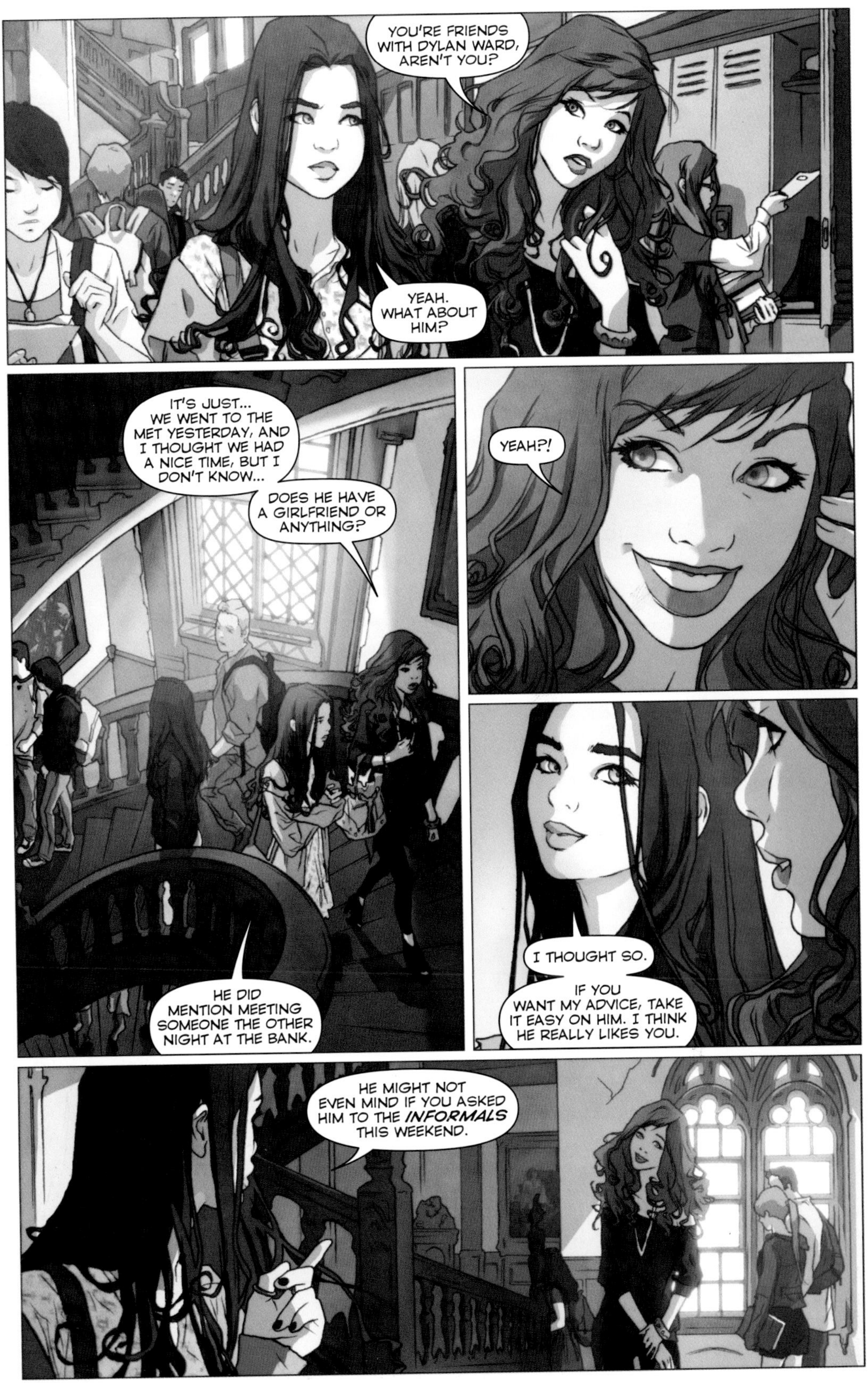
YOU'RE FRIENDS WITH DYLAN WARD, AREN'T YOU?
YEAH. WHAT ABOUT HIM?
IT'S JUST... WE WENT TO THE MET YESTERDAY, AND I THOUGHT WE HAD A NICE TIME, BUT I DON'T KNOW...
DOES HE HAVE A GIRLFRIEND OR ANYTHING?
HE DID MENTION MEETING SOMEONE THE OTHER NIGHT AT THE BANK.
YEAH?!
I THOUGHT SO.
IF YOU WANT MY ADVICE, TAKE IT EASY ON HIM. I THINK HE REALLY LIKES YOU.
HE MIGHT NOT EVEN MIND IF YOU ASKED HIM TO THE *INFORMALS* THIS WEEKEND.

SATURDAY NIGHT.

CLICK

CLICK

IT'S BEAUTIFUL, OLLIE.

WHERE DID YOU GET IT?

OH, YOU CAN HAVE ANYTHING DELIVERED IN NEW YORK.

WELL, HOW DO WE LOOK?

PERFECT.

SHALL WE?

WE SHALL.

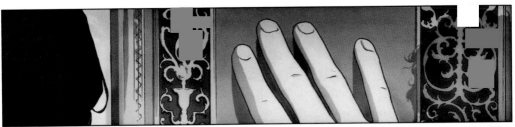

NICE *DRESS*. WHO'S SHE WEARING, MARC JACOBS?

MORE LIKE *SALVATION ARMY.*

NEVER MIND THEM. CHECK OUT DYLAN.

THANKS TO YOU, *LITTLE MISS MATCHMAKER*, HE'S HANGING WITH ONE OF THE MIMI CLONES.

OUR TRI-O'S DOWN TO TWO...

OR IT COULD BE A *QUARTET*.

I DON'T GET THE SENSE THAT SHE'S INTO ALL OF THAT "TEAM FORCE" GARBAGE.

YOU HAVE TO GIVE HIM CREDIT.

WE'VE KNOWN THESE PEOPLE MOST OF OUR LIVES AND WE'RE STILL OUTSIDERS.

DYLAN TRANSFERS A *FEW WEEKS* AGO AND ALREADY HE'S FOUND A PLACE FOR HIMSELF.

WE'LL ALWAYS HAVE EACH OTHER.

WANNA DANCE?

NAH. LET'S JUST GO.

WELL, LOOK WHO'S DECIDED TO *GRACE* US WITH HIS PRESENCE.

LEAVING ALREADY?

WE WERE JUST ABOUT TO.

YOU SHOULD STAY. YOU MIGHT ENJOY IT.

C'MON, SKY. I'LL CATCH US A CAB.

I...UH...

I'LL SEE YOU LATER, OLLIE... ALL RIGHT?

COME ON.

WH-WHAT'S HAPPENING TO THE ROOM? TO *EVERYONE?*

DON'T YOU *SEE* IT?

DON'T BE AFRAID.

SURRENDER TO IT.

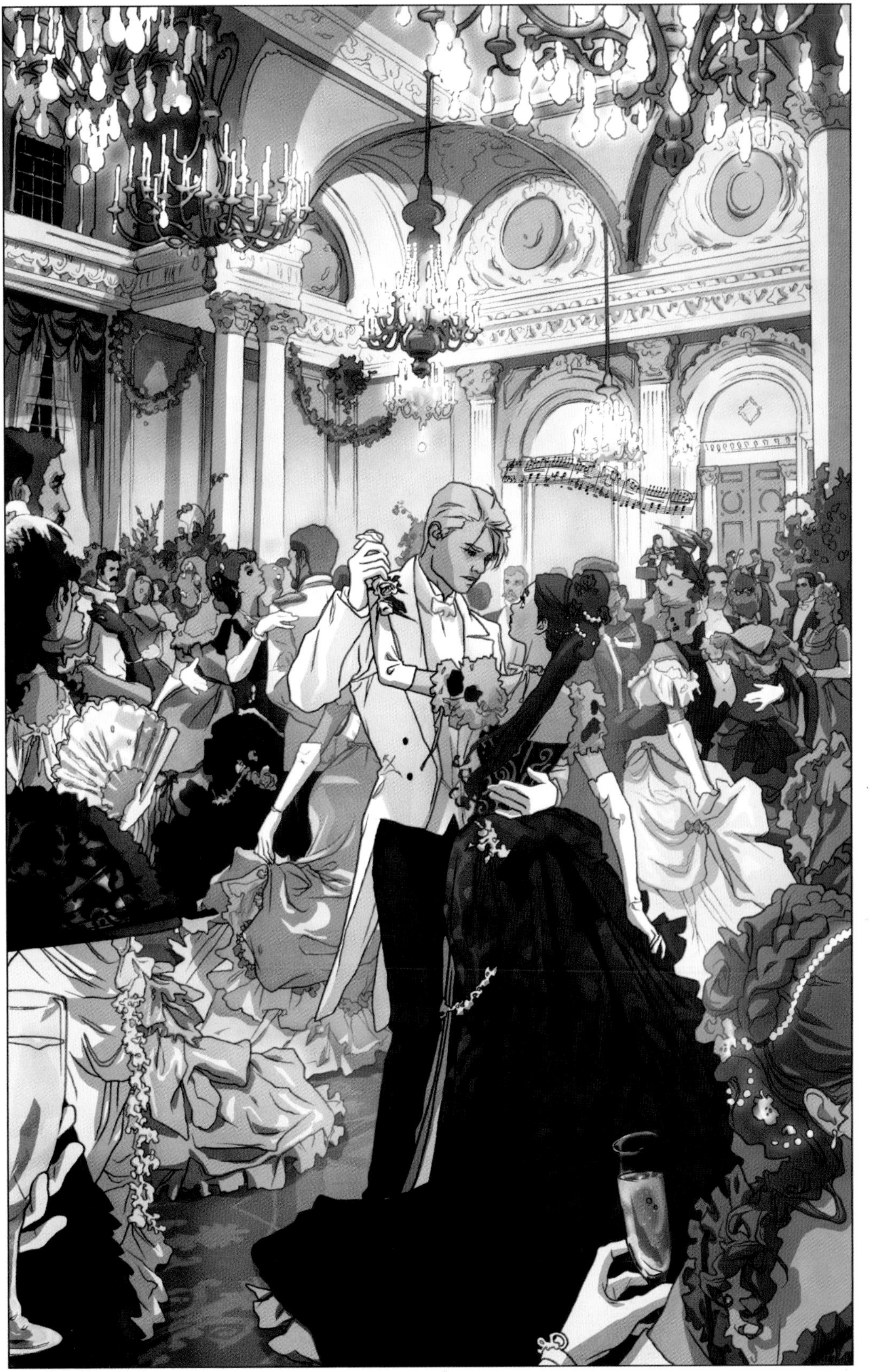

IT HAPPENED JUST LIKE THAT.

WHEN THE SONG WAS OVER, THE ROOM WAS BACK TO NORMAL. LIKE I *DAYDREAMED* IT OR SOMETHING.

FSSHT

AND THE BOY...*JACK FORCE*. I DON'T KNOW WHAT TO MAKE OF HIM, EITHER.

HE LOOKS AT ME LIKE HE KNOWS ME, BUT WE'VE HARDLY EVEN TALKED TO EACH OTHER.

FSSHT

BOYS, RIGHT?

WHO CAN FIGURE THEM OUT?

FSSHT

FSSHT

FSSHT

ANYWAY, I JUST WANTED TO TALK TO YOU ABOUT IT.

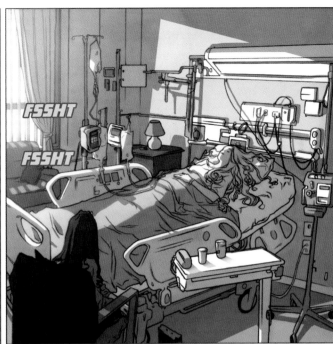

FSSHT

FSSHT

FSSHT

I'D BETTER GO.

THERE'S SOME *SOCIAL CLUB* THAT CORDELIA WANTS ME TO JOIN TOMORROW, AND I STILL HAVEN'T FILLED OUT THE PAPERWORK.

FSSHT

TRY TO WAKE UP SOON, OKAY?

FSSHT

SEE YOU NEXT WEEKEND, MOM.

huff
huff

I *huff* THINK IT'S ALL THERE *huff* MRS. DUPONT.

HOW'D *SHE* GET AN INVITE?

YOU AS THRILLED TO BE HERE AS I AM?

pfft TOTALLY.

WELCOME TO THIS SEASON'S FIRST MEETING OF THE NEW YORK BLOOD BANK COMMITTEE.

WE ARE VERY PROUD TO HAVE YOU HERE.

AS YOU ALREADY KNOW, THE COMMITTEE IS ONE OF THE PREMIER PHILANTHROPIC ORGANIZATIONS IN THE NORTHEAST.

OUR FUND-RAISING EFFORTS BUILD HOSPITALS, FOUND INSTITUTIONS, AND SPONSOR RESEARCH INTO BLOODBORNE DISEASES.

WHENEVER CUTTING-EDGE SCIENCE CONFRONTS MEDICAL NEED, THE COMMITTEE IS THERE.

BUT HELPING OTHERS IS NOT *ALL* THAT THE COMMITTEE DOES.

YOU HAVE BEEN ASKED HERE BECAUSE YOU ARE VERY SPECIAL. AND BECAUSE YOU ALL SHARE SOMETHING IN COMMON.

SOME OF YOU MIGHT HAVE NOTICED CERTAIN CHANGES IN YOUR BODIES.

BLUE MARKS ON YOUR ARMS, PERHAPS. THIS IS THE *SANGRE AZUL*, THE BLOOD THAT MARKS US AS OUR KIND.

OTHERS OF YOU MIGHT HAVE FOUND THAT YOU ARE SUDDENLY ABLE TO DO THINGS VERY WELL, EXCELLING IN TESTS YOU HAVE NOT STUDIED FOR.

OR THAT YOU CAN EAT ANYTHING YOU WANT, AS MUCH AS YOU WANT, AND STILL NOT GAIN AN OUNCE.

HAS ANYONE NOTICED THE SENSATION OF *TIME* SLOWING DOWN, OR EVEN SLIPPING AWAY?

ALL OF THIS IS NORMAL. *YOU* ARE NORMAL.

LIKE ME, LIKE MANY OF YOUR CLASSMATES, LIKE YOUR PARENTS, GRANDPARENTS, SIBLINGS, AND RELATIVES, YOU ARE PART OF THE LONG AND NOBLE TRADITION OF THE FOUR HUNDRED.

TODAY IS YOUR INDUCTION INTO YOUR SECRET HISTORY.

YOU ARE THE NEWEST *BLUE BLOODS*.

YOU ARE--

SCHUYLER, WAIT!

VAMPIRES?!? YOU'RE ALL CERTIFIABLY NUTS!

IT'S NOT LIKE THAT. WE'RE NOT B-MOVIE BLOODSUCKERS. WE'RE--

I HEARD MRS. DUPONT. YOU'RE *FALLEN ANGELS* TRYING TO EARN YOUR WAY BACK INTO HEAVEN BY THROWING FUND-RAISERS.

THAT'S SO MUCH MORE BELIEVABLE.

IF YOU DON'T WANT TO BELIEVE YOUR EARS, WHAT ABOUT YOUR EYES?

YOU MUST'VE SEEN THE LINES ON YOUR ARMS.

THE *SANGRE AZUL* SHINES THROUGH OUR SKIN BECAUSE IT'S ASSERTING ITSELF.

IT CONNECTS US TO THE KNOWLEDGE AND MEMORIES OF OUR PAST LIVES.

OUR BLOOD HAS BEEN ALIVE SINCE THE BEGINNING OF TIME.

THE OTHER NIGHT AT THE DANCE, REMEMBER?

WE SAW OURSELVES IN A DIFFERENT TIME BECAUSE WE'VE *LIVED* IN A DIFFERENT TIME.

THAT'S JUST ONE OF OUR GIFTS. SOME OF US HAVE SUPERSTRENGTH, OTHERS CAN DO MIND CONTROL.

THERE ARE EVEN SHAPE-SHIFTERS, BUT THAT'S NOT AS COMMON.

IT DOESN'T MAKE ANY SENSE. I MEAN, I REALIZE I DON'T HAVE THE BEST TAN, BUT IT'S NOT LIKE THE SUN *HURTS ME* OR ANYTHING.

AND I LOVE ITALIAN FOOD.

GARLIC, SUNLIGHT, WOODEN STAKES...THOSE ARE ALL JUST MYTHS *WE* CREATED TO THROW THE RED BLOODS A CURVEBALL.

RED BLOODS? YOU MEAN *PEOPLE*.

AND YOU, LIKE, *EAT* THEM?

IT'S NOT LIKE THAT. I MEAN, WE *DO* DRINK THEIR BLOOD, BUT IT DOESN'T HURT THEM. THEY DON'T EVEN REMEMBER WHAT HAPPENED.

AND WE *NEVER* KILL THEM. THAT GOES AGAINST THE CODE OF THE VAMPIRES.

IT'S THE MOST IMPORTANT RULE OF ALL.

EVEN IF I BELIEVED YOU-- WHICH I *DON'T*-- I KNOW I'M NOT ONE OF YOU.

I KNOW *I'M* NOT A VAMPIRE.

PUT YOUR FINGER IN YOUR MOUTH.

YOU SHOULD FEEL THEM RIGHT HERE.

FEEL WHAT? MY *MOLARS?*

JUST *CONCENTRATE.*

YOU CAN CONTROL WHEN THEY EXTEND AND RETRACT.

I *AM* CONCENTRATING. THIS IS ME CONCEN--

OUCH!

DO YOU BELIEVE ME *NOW?*

I WAS SO WORRIED I WAS GOING CRAZY.

THE *DREAMS* I'VE BEEN HAVING...

IN ONE I WAS IN ANCIENT EGYPT. I SAW *YOU* IN ANOTHER ONE.

REALLY? WHAT WAS I WEARING?

A GINGHAM DRESS, I THINK.

FASHION EMERGENCY!

I WISH I COULD *FORGET* THAT ONE!

AS YOUR BLOOD GETS STRONGER, YOU'LL BE ABLE TO ACCESS MORE MEMORIES. I'VE SEEN YOU, TOO.

I'VE SEEN *EVERYONE* AT ONE TIME OR ANOTHER. EXCEPT THAT VAN ALEN *FREAK*.

I WAS SURPRISED TO SEE HER AT THE MEETING. *NO WAY* WOULD I HAVE THOUGHT SHE COULD BE WITH US.

HOW MANY OF *US* ARE THERE?

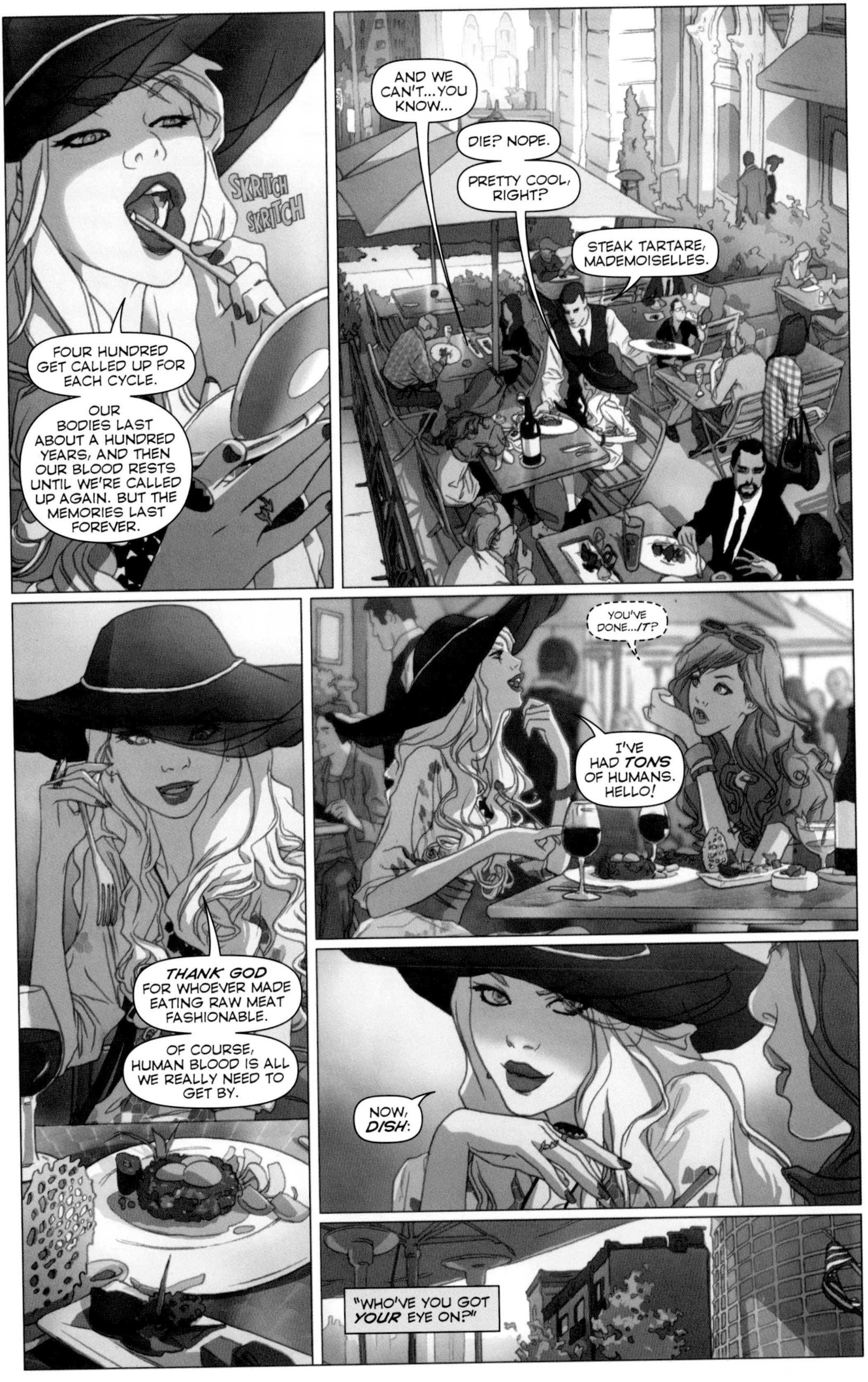
SKRITCH SKRITCH
FOUR HUNDRED GET CALLED UP FOR EACH CYCLE.
OUR BODIES LAST ABOUT A HUNDRED YEARS, AND THEN OUR BLOOD RESTS UNTIL WE'RE CALLED UP AGAIN. BUT THE MEMORIES LAST FOREVER.
AND WE CAN'T...YOU KNOW...
DIE? NOPE.
PRETTY COOL, RIGHT?
STEAK TARTARE, MADEMOISELLES.
THANK GOD FOR WHOEVER MADE EATING RAW MEAT FASHIONABLE.
OF COURSE, HUMAN BLOOD IS ALL WE REALLY NEED TO GET BY.
YOU'VE DONE...*IT*?
I'VE HAD *TONS* OF HUMANS. HELLO!
NOW, *DISH*:
"WHO'VE YOU GOT *YOUR* EYE ON?"

SCHUYLER...?

I DIDN'T THINK WE'D SEE YOU AGAIN UNTIL THE WEEKEND.

ENOUGH!

I WANT YOU TO TELL ME!

WHO AM I? WAS MY FATHER A VAMPIRE? DID HE DO THIS TO YOU?

IS *HE* THE REASON I'M A *MONSTER?*

PLEASE ⸢sob⸣ I HAVE TO KNOW.

I SUSPECTED YOU WOULD COME HERE FIRST.

YOU *KNEW*. WHY DIDN'T YOU TELL ME?

THE BURDEN OF KNOWING ONESELF SHOULDN'T BE CAST UNTIL YOU ARE READY.

IT IS NOT OUR WAY.

OUR WAY? YOU MEAN, YOU--

OF COURSE, CHILD. IT ISN'T YOUR FATHER WHO IS RESPONSIBLE FOR YOUR BLOODLINE.

YOUR *MOTHER* IS THE "MONSTER" WE ALL ARE.

WHAT?

IF SHE'S AN ALL-POWERFUL VAMPIRE, THEN WHY'S SHE IN A COMA?

YOUR MOTHER HAS MADE SOME UNFORTUNATE CHOICES IN HER LIFE.

BUT WHATEVER SHE HAS DONE, DO NOT DOUBT THAT YOU ARE *PRIVILEGED* TO HAVE HER HERITAGE.

ARE YOU REALLY MY GRANDMOTHER?

TECHNICALLY, NO.

WHEN OUR BODIES EXPIRE, A SINGLE DROP OF OUR BLOOD IS LEFT BEHIND WITH OUR DNA PATTERN.

WHEN IT IS TIME TO RELEASE A NEW SPIRIT, THOSE OF US WHO CHOOSE TO CARRY ARE IMPLANTED WITH THE NEW LIFE.

SO IN A WAY, WE ARE BOTH RELATED AND NOT RELATED AT ALL. BUT YOU *ARE* MY CHARGE AND RESPONSIBILITY.

AND MY FATHER?

HE IS OF NO CONCERN TO YOU.

HE IS *GONE*, AND THAT IS ALL YOU NEED TO KNOW.

THIS IS A HARD TIME FOR OUR KIND. FULL OF VULGARITY AND DESPAIR.

WE ARE CREATURES OF BEAUTY AND LIGHT, AND WE HAVE TRIED OUR BEST TO INFLUENCE THE WORLD. BUT THE RED BLOODS ARE TOO MANY, AND WE ARE TOO FEW.

THERE ARE FEWER AND FEWER OF US WHO CHOOSE TO GO THROUGH THE PROPER CYCLES.

OUR WAY OF LIFE--OUR VALUES-- ARE QUICKLY DISAPPEARING.

MANY HAVE LOST HOPE THAT WE WILL EVER REACH THE EXALTED STATE AND REGAIN THE KINGDOM OF HEAVEN.

IMMORTALITY IS A *BLESSING* AND A *CURSE.*

I HAVE LIVED THROUGH TOO MUCH.

NOW THAT YOU KNOW THE TRUTH, CHILD, YOU MUST PREPARE.

A *DARKNESS* IS COMING.

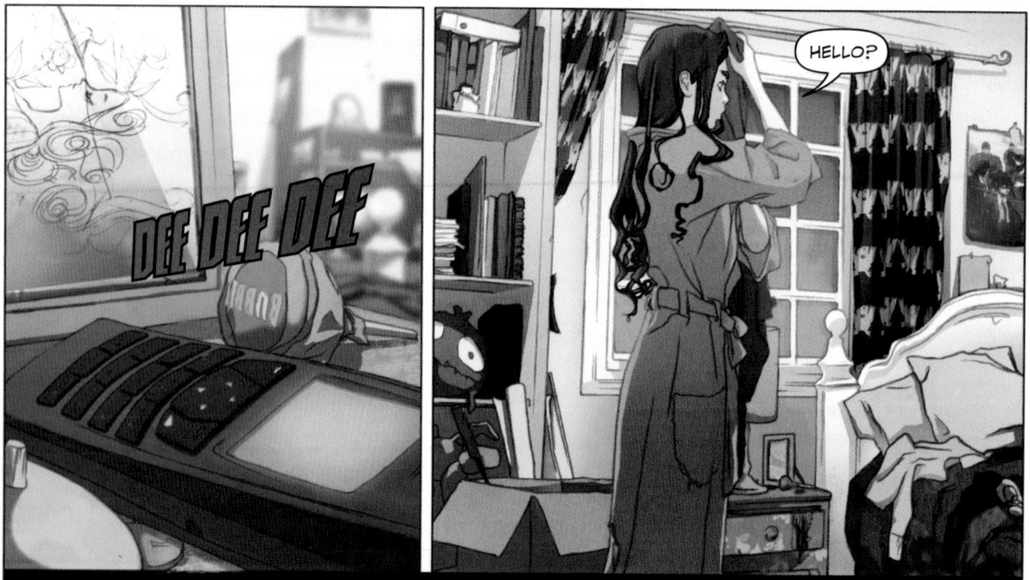
DEE DEE DEE
HELLO?

PART III: THE HUNT

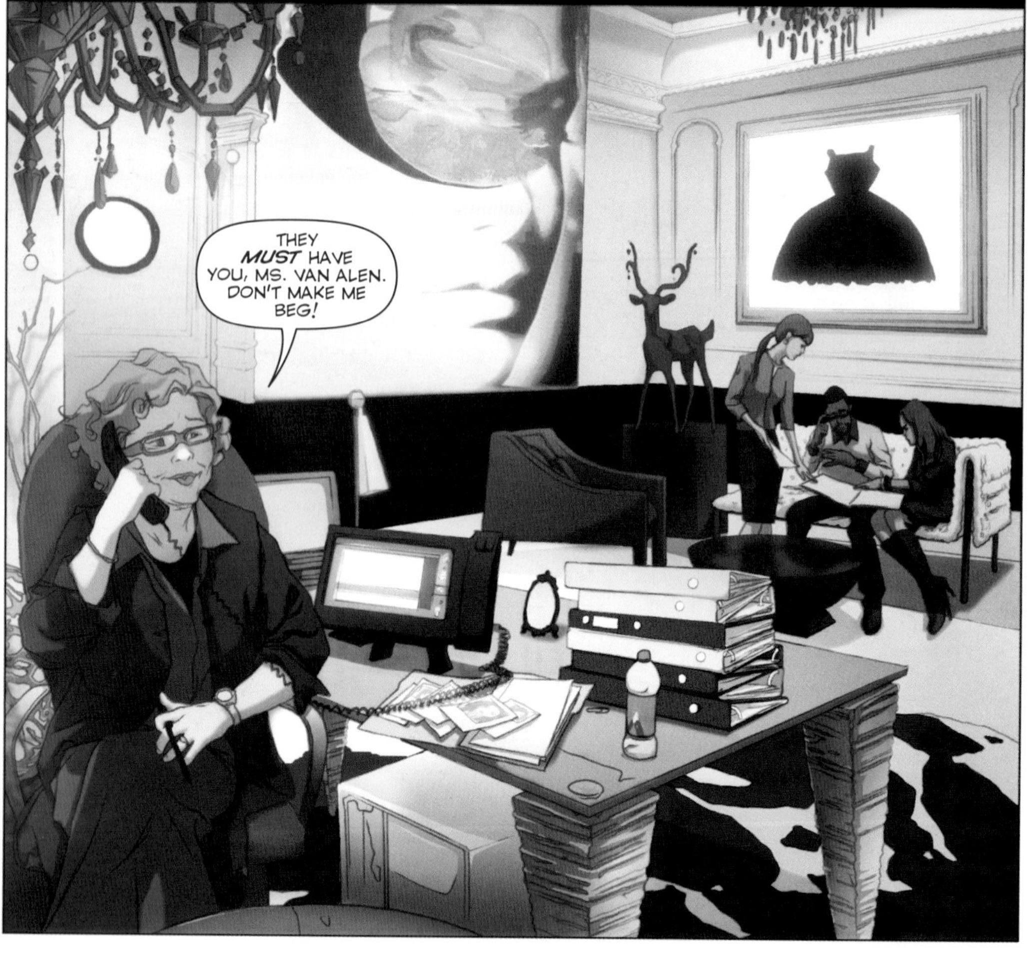
THEY *MUST* HAVE YOU, MS. VAN ALEN. DON'T MAKE ME BEG!

STITCHED BY CIVILIZATION

NO LOITERING! WE NEED YOU IN HAIR AND MAKEUP!

I'M SORRY WE CALLED YOU IN SO LAST MINUTE, BUT THAT'S THE BIZ.

OH...UH...NO PROBLEM.

MEET LEON AND PERFECTION. THEY'LL FIX YOU UP.

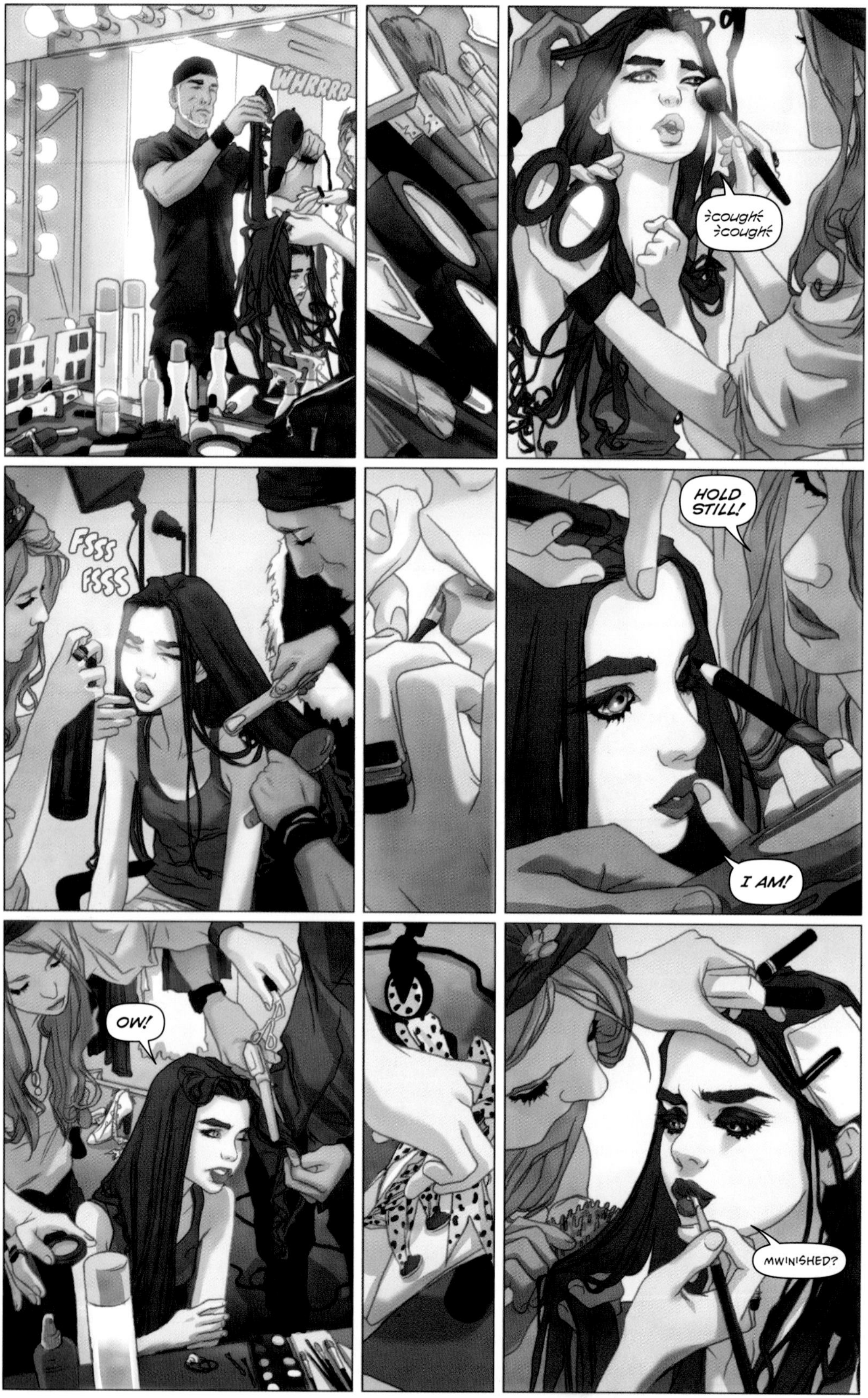

WHRRRR
cough cough
FSSS FSSS
HOLD STILL!
I AM!
OW!
MWINISHED?

OH, MY...

YOU LOOK *SO* GREAT.

THANKS. I FEEL SO *SILLY*.

I'M GLAD THERE ARE TWO NEW FACES OF CIVILIZATION. I DON'T THINK I COULD HANDLE THIS ALONE.

LET'S GO TO WORK. THE METER'S RUNNING.

CLEAR THE SET, PEOPLE! TIME TO LIGHT THIS CANDLE.

NOW, GIVE ME *FIRE*, GIRLS.

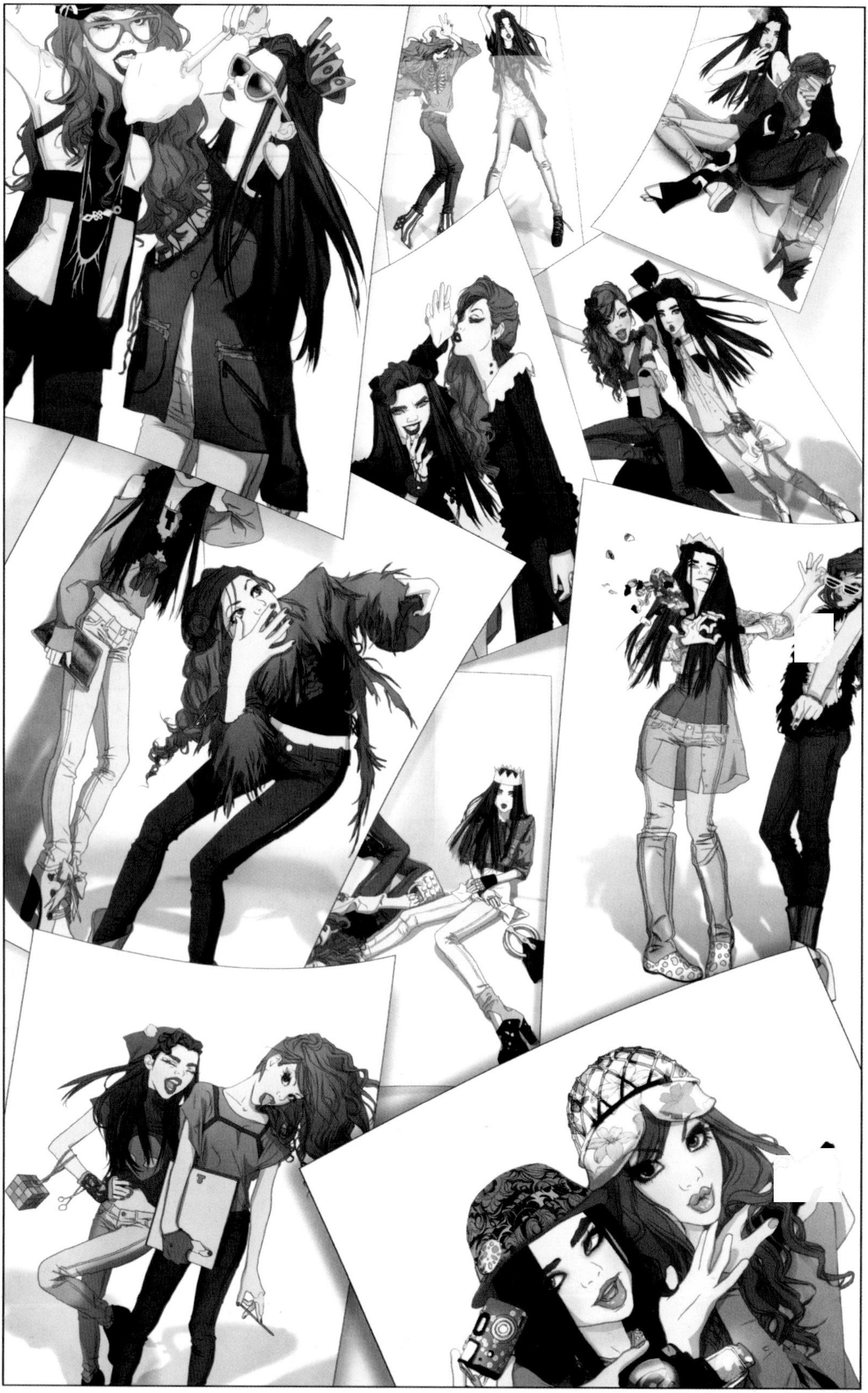

I CAN SEE WHY DYLAN LIKES YOU. YOU'RE NOTHING LIKE--

MIMI?

WHAT CAN I SAY...OUR FATHERS ARE FRIENDS, SO WE JUST ENDED UP THAT WAY, TOO.

NEVER IN A *MILLION YEARS* DID I THINK I'D SAY THIS, BUT THAT WAS REALLY COOL.

YEAH. EXACTLY WHAT WE NEEDED AFTER THIS WEEK'S DRAMA.

SHE'S GOING TO *DIE* WHEN SHE HEARS WE GOT PICKED FOR THE AD CAMPAIGN AND NOT HER.

IF ONLY SHE *COULD* DIE.

HAHAHAHAHA

YOU WANT A LIFT? MY RIDE WILL BE HERE IN A SEC.

NO THANKS. I'M GOING TO WALK.

SEE YOU LATER!

CLINK
CLINK

BLISS?
IS THAT--

≷gasp≷

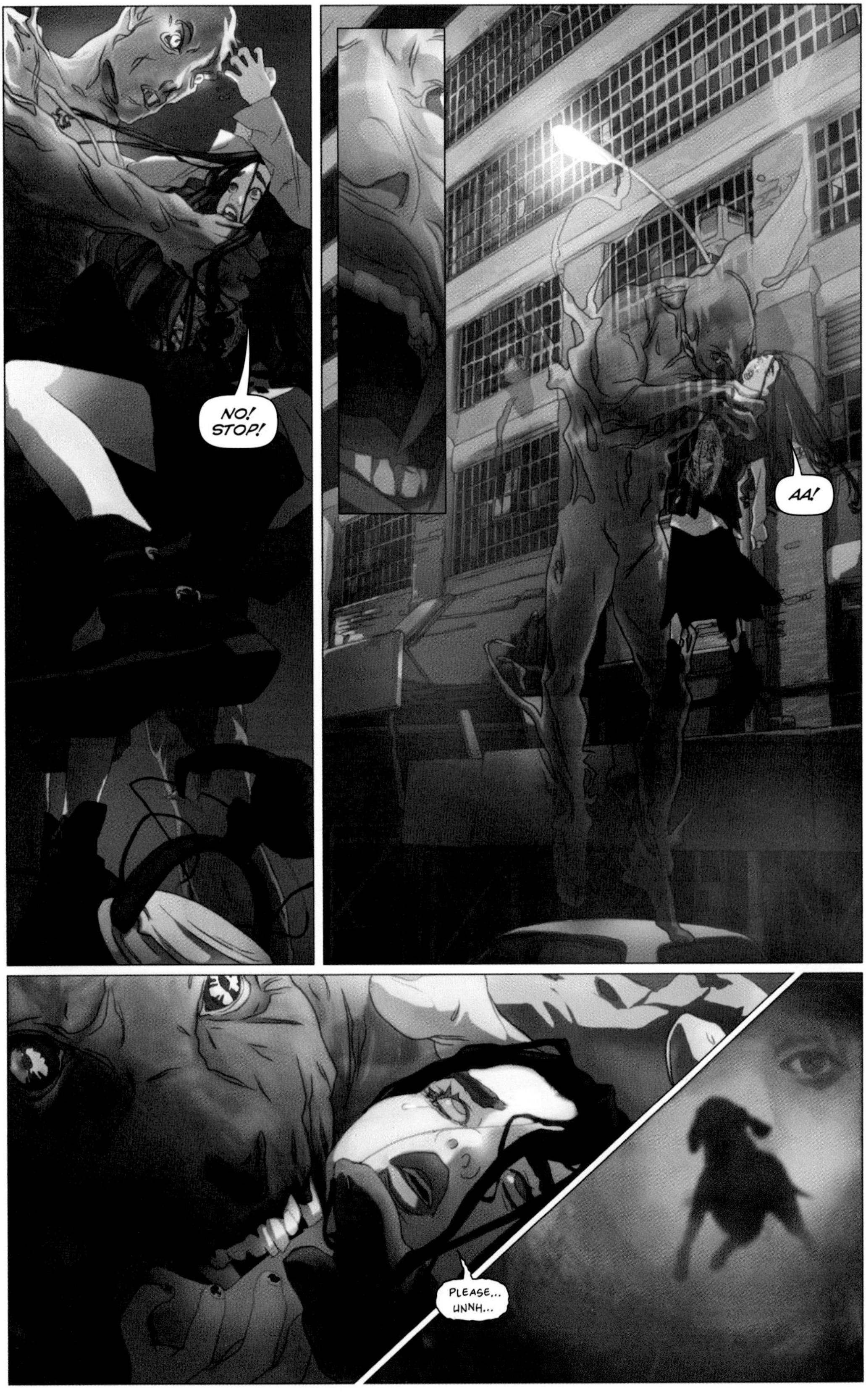
NO! STOP!
AA!
PLEASE... UNNH...

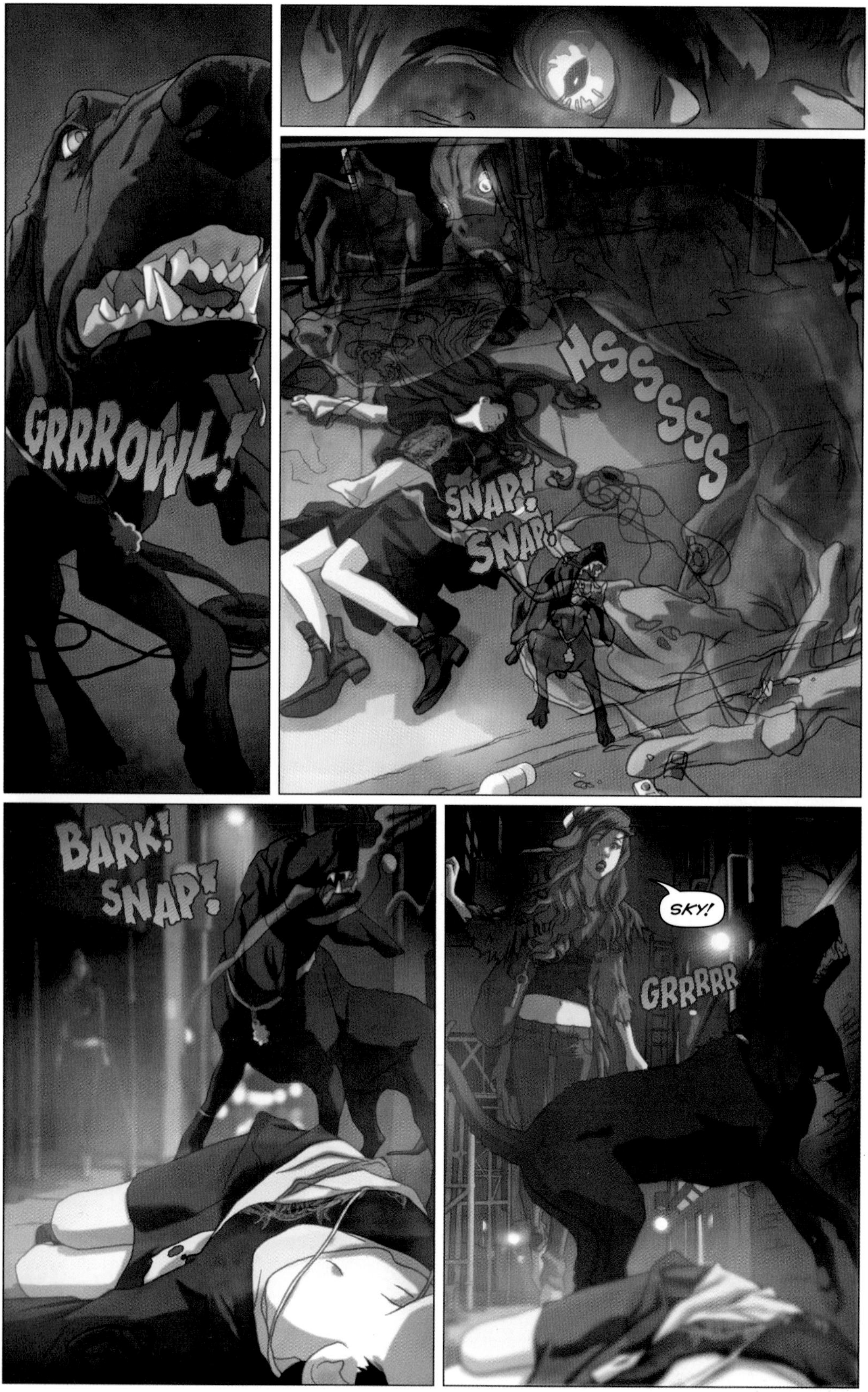
GRRROWL!
HSSSSSS
SNAP!
SNAP!
BARK!
SNAP!
SKY!
GRRRRR

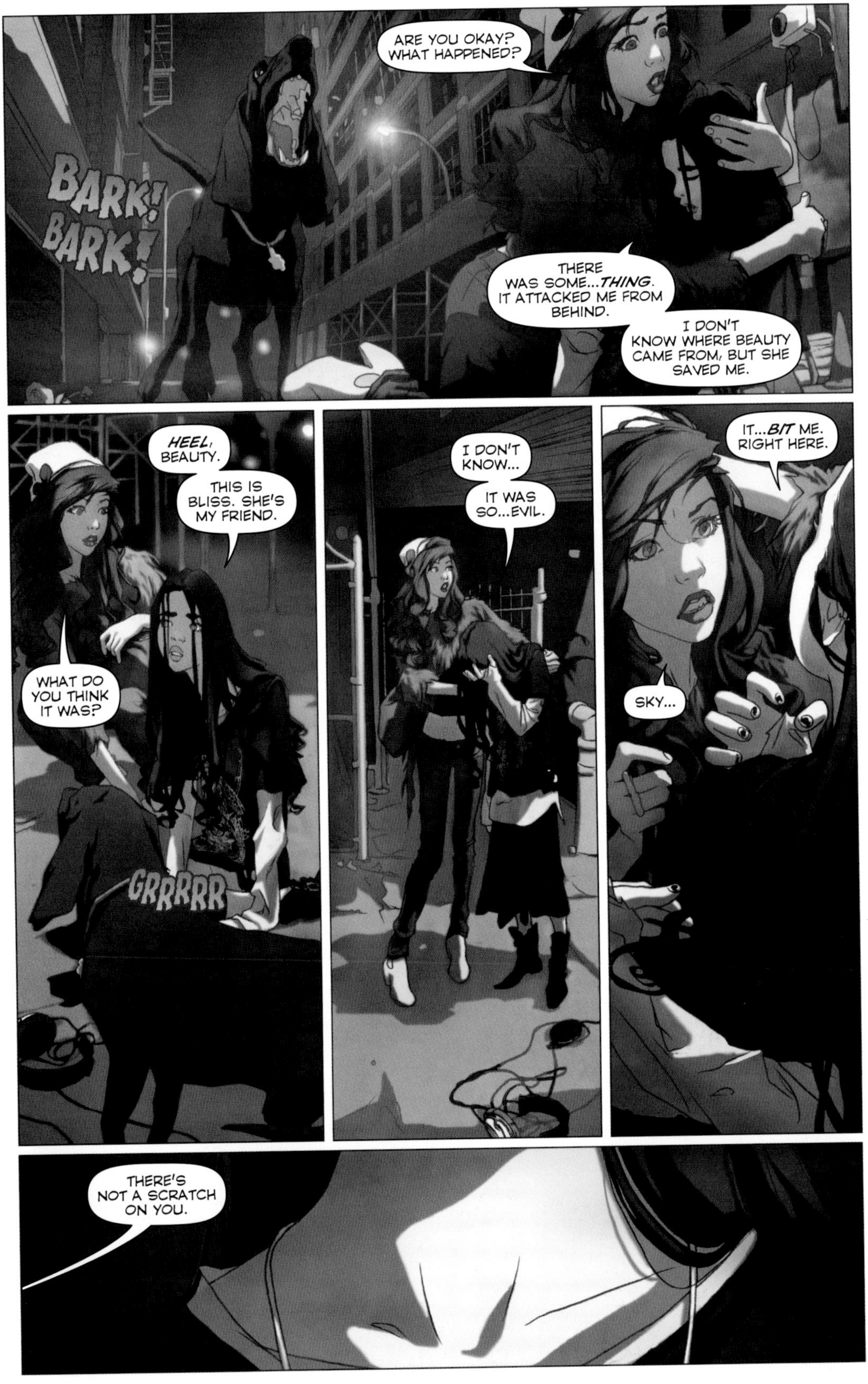
ARE YOU OKAY? WHAT HAPPENED?
BARK! BARK!
THERE WAS SOME...*THING*. IT ATTACKED ME FROM BEHIND.
I DON'T KNOW WHERE BEAUTY CAME FROM, BUT SHE SAVED ME.
HEEL, BEAUTY.
THIS IS BLISS. SHE'S MY FRIEND.
WHAT DO YOU THINK IT WAS?
GRRRRR
I DON'T KNOW...
IT WAS SO...EVIL.
IT...*BIT* ME. RIGHT HERE.
SKY...
THERE'S NOT A SCRATCH ON YOU.

THE BANK.

THIRSTY?

WHAT'S IT TO YOU?

DOUBLE-FISTING ISN'T VERY LADYLIKE.

I'M ONLY A LADY WHEN I *HAVE* TO BE.

SO, WHERE'S BLISS?

I THOUGHT YOU TWO WERE ATTACHED AT THE *PELVIS*.

SHE'LL BE HERE LATER.

BUT I'M HERE *NOW*.

SCHUYLER! WHAT'S WRONG?

DYLAN'S TEXT SAID HE'D BE HERE. I'D BETTER FIND HIM.

TELL ME.

RED EYES... FANGS...

I FELT THEM, DEEP IN MY VEINS. BUT THERE'S NO MARK. I DON'T UNDERSTAND.

SIT DOWN.

THERE'S SOMETHING I NEED TO TELL YOU.

WE DON'T DIE, THAT'S TRUE.

BUT WE *CAN* BE KILLED.

SOMETHING IS OUT THERE HUNTING BLUE BLOODS.

I WASN'T SURE BEFORE, BUT I AM NOW.

DON'T YOU HAVE THAT BACKWARD?

I THOUGHT *WE* WERE THE HUNTERS. THE COMMITTEE SAID WE CAN'T DIE.

AGGIE WAS ONE OF US, SCHUYLER. A BLUE BLOOD.

WHEN THEY FOUND HER, ALL OF HER BLOOD WAS DRAINED FROM HER BODY. TOTAL CONSUMPTION.

HER MEMORIES, HER PAST LIVES, HER SOUL...ALL GONE. *TAKEN*.

THE COMMITTEE IS HOLDING BACK SOMETHING ABOUT OUR HISTORY. I THINK IT HAS TO DO WITH PLYMOUTH, WHEN WE FIRST CAME HERE.

I'VE TRIED TO ACCESS MY MEMORIES, BUT IT'S LIKE THEY'VE BEEN TAMPERED WITH SOMEHOW. ALL I COME UP WITH IS ONE WORD: "CROATAN."

"CROATAN"?

WHAT'S THAT?

I DON'T KNOW. BUT WHATEVER IT IS--

"--IT'S BACK."

JUST RELAX, SWEETIE.

THIS WON'T HURT A BIT.

WH-WHAT'RE YOU DOING?

I WAS ABOUT TO ASK THE *SAME* QUESTION.

BLISS, THERE YOU ARE!

WE WERE JUST TALKING.

LOOKED LIKE A PRETTY *POINTED* CONVERSATION.

LET'S GO, DYLAN.

shuff

WAIT! YOU'RE *LEAVING?*

I SHOULDN'T HAVE SAID ANYTHING.

IT'S GOING TO BE DANGEROUS, POKING AROUND LOOKING FOR ANSWERS. I DON'T WANT YOU GETTING HURT.

THE DOGS ARE OUR GUARDIANS. THEY PROTECT US WHILE WE MAKE THE CHANGE FROM HUMAN TO BLUE BLOOD.

YOU SHOULDN'T GO ANYWHERE WITHOUT HER.

IT'S TOO LATE FOR THAT. I COULD'VE ENDED UP LIKE AGGIE TONIGHT, REMEMBER?

SOMEHOW, MY BLOODHOUND KNEW I WAS IN TROUBLE. OTHERWISE, *I* WOULD'VE BEEN DRAINED.

YOU SHOULDN'T BE ALONE, EITHER.

IF IT'S GOING TO BE DANGEROUS, THEN YOU'LL NEED ALL THE HELP--

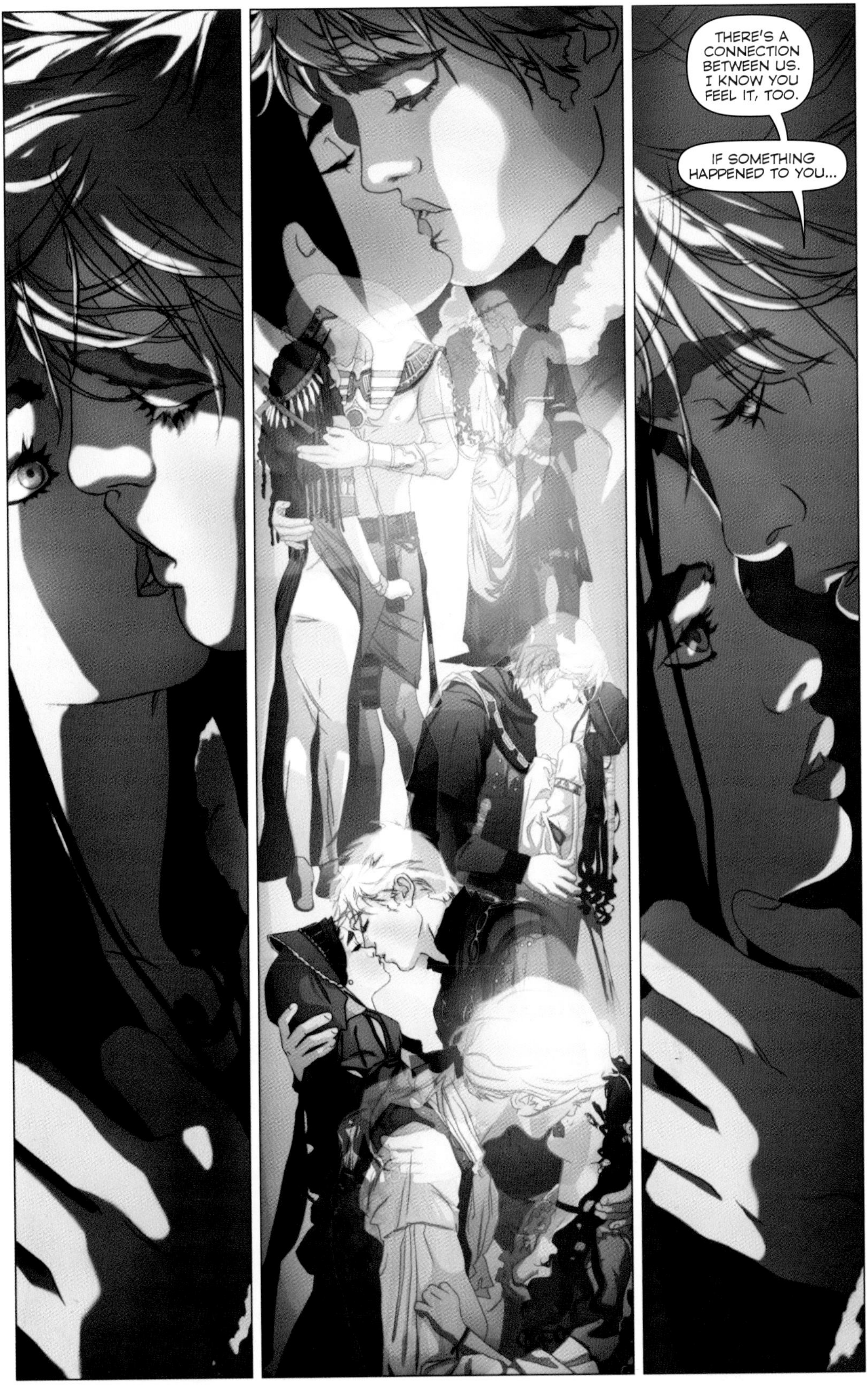
THERE'S A CONNECTION BETWEEN US. I KNOW YOU FEEL IT, TOO.
IF SOMETHING HAPPENED TO YOU...

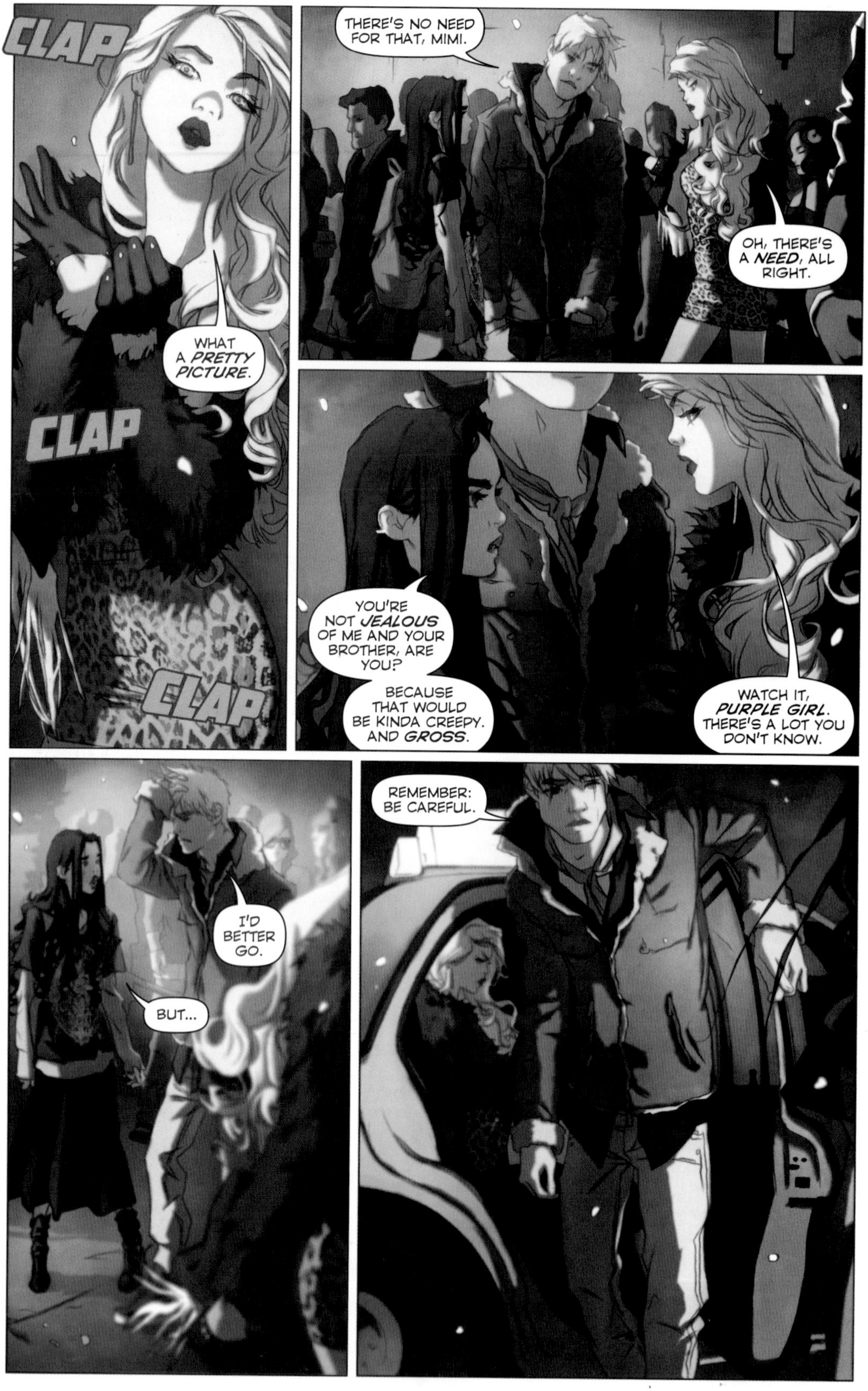
CLAP
WHAT A *PRETTY PICTURE*.
CLAP
CLAP
THERE'S NO NEED FOR THAT, MIMI.
OH, THERE'S A *NEED*, ALL RIGHT.
YOU'RE NOT *JEALOUS* OF ME AND YOUR BROTHER, ARE YOU?
BECAUSE THAT WOULD BE KINDA CREEPY. AND *GROSS*.
WATCH IT, *PURPLE GIRL*. THERE'S A LOT YOU DON'T KNOW.
I'D BETTER GO.
BUT...
REMEMBER: BE CAREFUL.

WELL, WELL.
TO WHAT DO I OWE
THIS HONOR?

WHAT'S THE
MATTER? YOUR NEW
BOYFRIEND NOT HERE
TO GET YOU IN WITH
A FIST BUMP?

HUH?

I'M
JUST SAYING, YOU
PROBABLY DON'T
WANT TO BE SEEN
WITH ME.

THERE'S BOUND TO
BE MUSIC INSIDE. PROBABLY
EVEN *DANCING.* ¿gasp¿

OH...

LOOK, OLLIE, I SHOULDN'T HAVE DITCHED YOU AT THE DANCE LIKE THAT. WE SHOWED UP TOGETHER, AND WE SHOULD'VE LEFT THAT WAY.

I'M REALLY SORRY.

SCHUYLER VAN ALEN ADMITTING SHE WAS WRONG.

WILL *WONDERS* NEVER CEASE.

SO WE'RE GOOD?

YEAH, WE'RE GOOD.

GOOD, BECAUSE WE NEED TO TALK.

I FOUND OUT SOMETHING ABOUT...ME. DON'T *FREAK*, OKAY?

SKY, I ALREADY KNOW.

WHAT?

C'MON INSIDE.

"LET ME SHOW YOU SOMETHING."

IT'S DOWN HERE.

THERE'S NOTHING BACK HERE.

JUST KEEP AN EYE OUT.

CL-CLACK

...

FOLLOW ME.

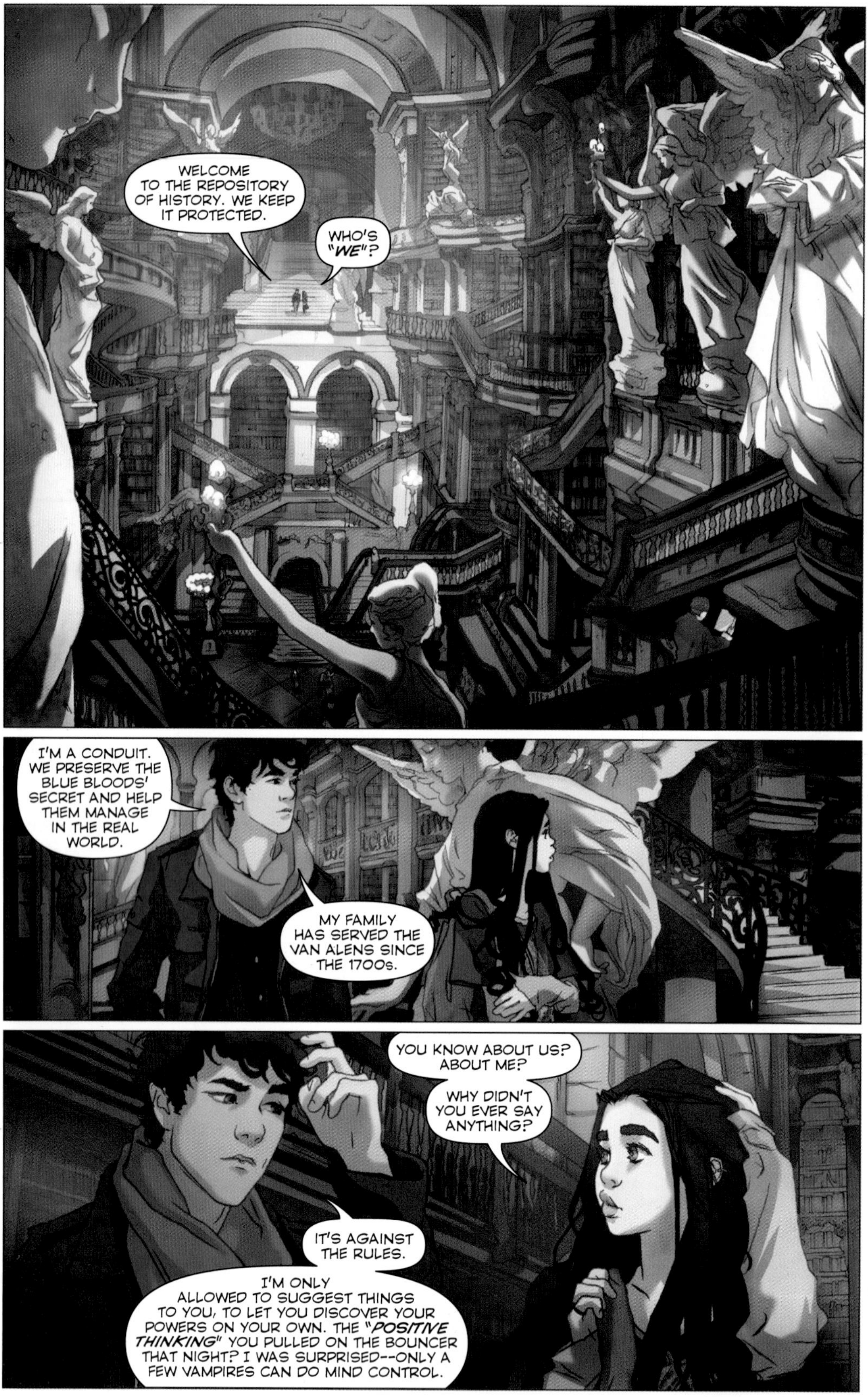
WELCOME TO THE REPOSITORY OF HISTORY. WE KEEP IT PROTECTED.
WHO'S "WE"?
I'M A CONDUIT. WE PRESERVE THE BLUE BLOODS' SECRET AND HELP THEM MANAGE IN THE REAL WORLD.
MY FAMILY HAS SERVED THE VAN ALENS SINCE THE 1700s.
YOU KNOW ABOUT US? ABOUT ME?
WHY DIDN'T YOU EVER SAY ANYTHING?
IT'S AGAINST THE RULES.
I'M ONLY ALLOWED TO SUGGEST THINGS TO YOU, TO LET YOU DISCOVER YOUR POWERS ON YOUR OWN. THE "POSITIVE THINKING" YOU PULLED ON THE BOUNCER THAT NIGHT? I WAS SURPRISED--ONLY A FEW VAMPIRES CAN DO MIND CONTROL.

"WHO ARE ALL OF THESE PEOPLE?"

"THE LIBRARIANS ARE CONDUITS WHO NO LONGER WORK FOR ANY SINGLE FAMILY.

"CONDUITS ARE AN ANCIENT TRADITION, BUT MOST BLUE BLOODS DON'T KEEP TO THE OLD WAYS."

THEY'D RATHER CONTROL THE RED BLOODS THAN LET US HELP.

SO...

MY BEST FRIEND IS REALLY, LIKE...MY BABYSITTER?

I AM YOUR FRIEND, SKY. BEING A CONDUIT HAS NOTHING TO DO WITH THAT.

GOOD THING. I'D HATE TO HAVE TO CHOW DOWN.

SO, NOW THAT THAT'S ALL STRAIGHTENED OUT...

...HOW WELL DO YOU KNOW YOUR WAY AROUND THIS PLACE?

SLAM!

IMPRESSIVE.

IT TOOK ME YEARS TO LEARN *FORCE PROJECTION*.

TELL HIM, FATHER!

TELL HIM ABOUT THE VAN ALEN *MONGREL*.

TELL ME WHAT? THAT YOU CAN'T STAND MY PAYING ATTENTION TO SOMEONE WHO *ISN'T YOU?*

I FIGURED THAT OUT ALL BY MYSELF.

YOU HAVEN'T FIGURED OUT *EVERYTHING*, BROTHER.

UNLIKE YOU, I'VE ACCESSED ALL OF MY MEMORIES, AND SHE'S NOT IN THEM. SHE ISN'T SUPPOSED TO EXIST.

DON'T BE RIDICULOUS. I SEE HER IN MINE.

RIGHT, FATHER?

BUT...I DON'T UNDERSTAND...

...WE CAN'T HAVE CHILDREN.

NOT AMONG OURSELVES. OUR EARTHLY BODIES ARE MERELY VESSELS THAT CARRY THE SPIRITS OF OUR KINDRED IN A NEW EMBRYONIC FORM.

BUT MISCEGENATION BETWEEN BLUE BLOODS AND RED BLOODS IS APPARENTLY NOT AS IMPOSSIBLE AS WE BELIEVED.

YOUR SISTER IS CORRECT. TECHNICALLY, SCHUYLER VAN ALEN ISN'T A BLUE BLOOD.

SHE IS THE PRODUCT OF THE *CAERIMONIA OSCULOR*-- A UNION BETWEEN A VAMPIRE AND A HUMAN FAMILIAR.

TO DO SUCH A THING... TO CONCEIVE A BABY OF MIXED BLOOD...

IT DEFIES THE *STRICTEST LAWS* OF OUR KIND. ALLEGRA VAN ALEN WAS A TROUBLED AND FOOLISH WOMAN.

MY MEMORIES... *HER* MEMORIES...?

THE FACE YOU'VE SEEN IS ALLEGRA'S, WHICH YOU UNDERSTANDABLY MISTOOK TO BE HER DAUGHTER'S. THE RESEMBLANCE *IS* STRIKING.

AND YOU MAY HAVE INADVERTENTLY PROJECTED YOUR OWN RECOLLECTIONS ONTO THE CHILD, SO SHE BELIEVED SHE WAS REMEMBERING THEM WITH YOU.

TOLD YOU. SHE'S A *MONGREL*.

WHAT'S GOING TO HAPPEN TO HER, THEN?

FOR NOW? NOTHING. THE CHILD APPEARS TO HAVE INHERITED SOME OF HER MOTHER'S ABILITIES, SO WE WILL WATCH AND WAIT. YOU SHOULD STAY CLEAR OF HER, HOWEVER.

NOW, AS TO THE MATTER OF *AUGUSTA'S DEATH*, WHICH YOUR SISTER TELLS ME IS ALSO OF CONCERN TO YOU--

--ALLOW ME TO EXPLAIN *THAT* AS WELL.

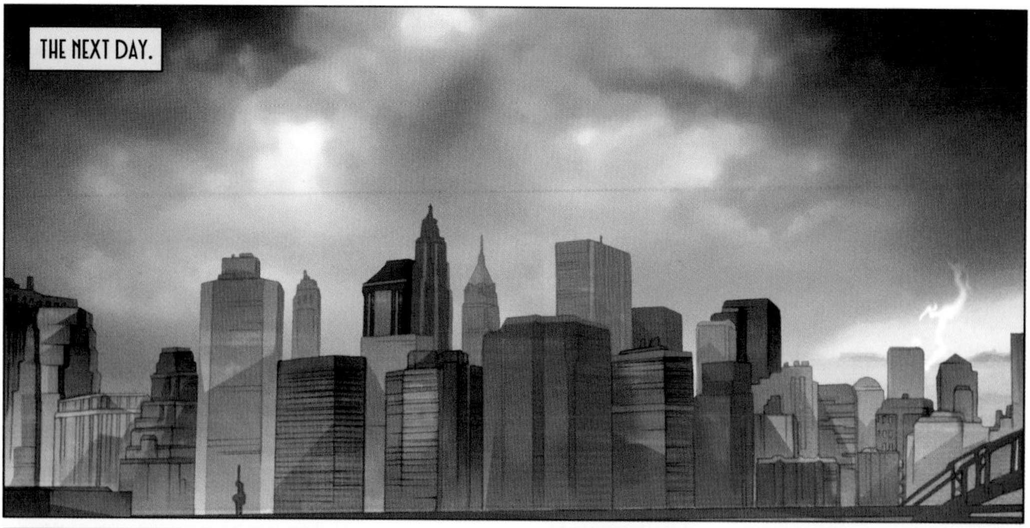
THE NEXT DAY.

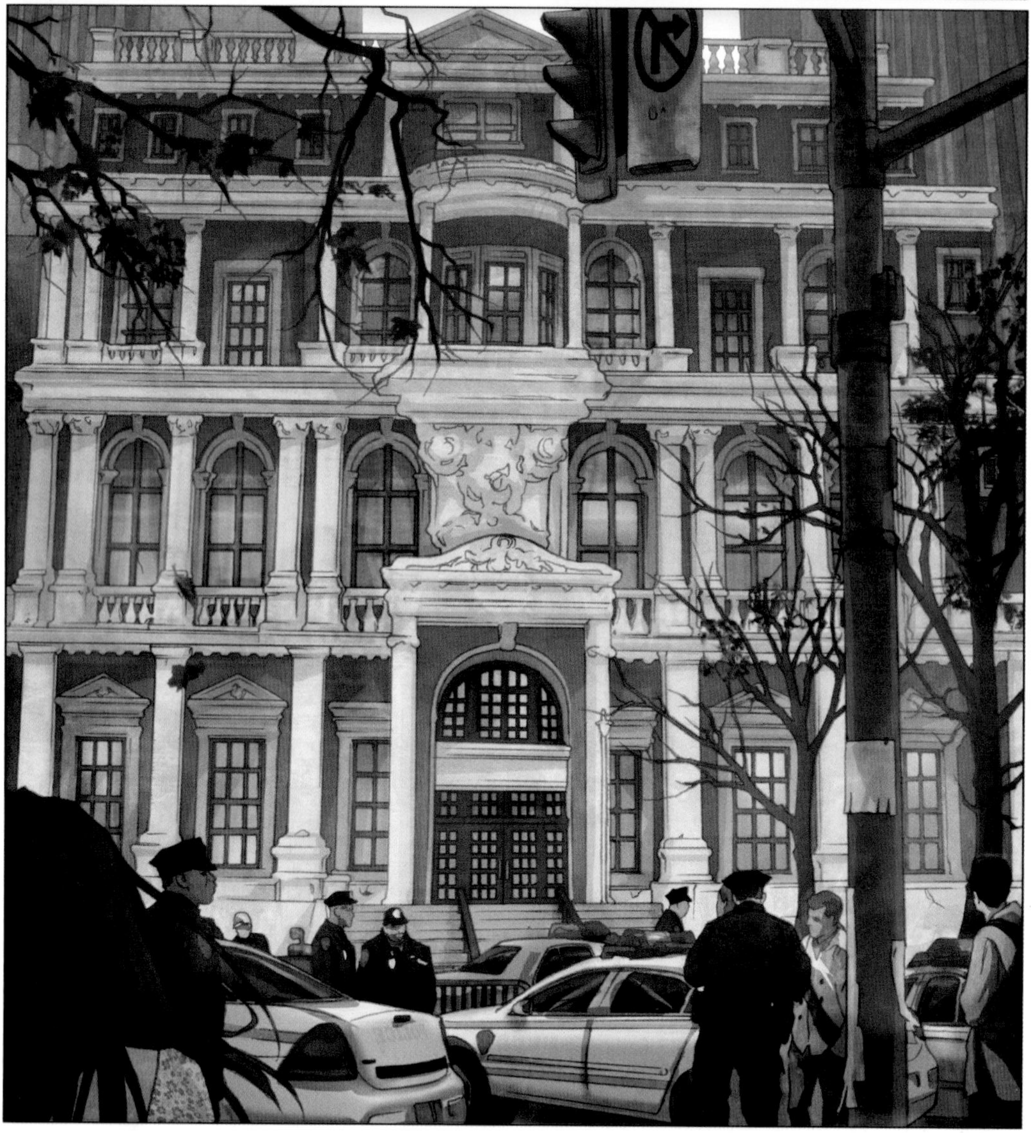

WHAT'S GOING ON?

NOT SURE. LOOKS LIKE BAD NEWS FOR SOMEONE.

DYLAN?!

WHAT IS THIS? WHY ARE THEY TAKING HIM AWAY?

IT'S A MISTAKE. IT *HAS* TO BE.

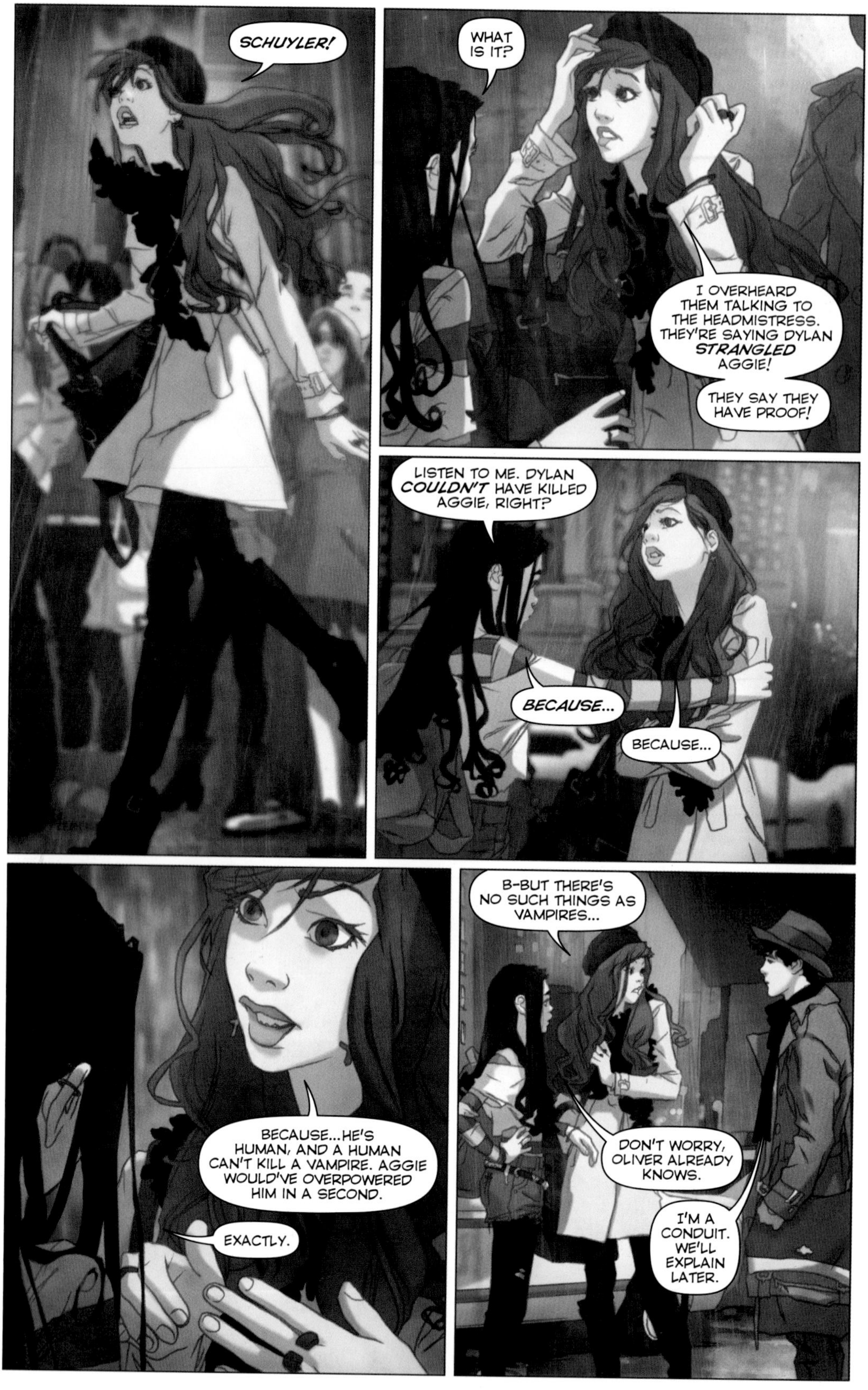
SCHUYLER!
WHAT IS IT?
I OVERHEARD THEM TALKING TO THE HEADMISTRESS. THEY'RE SAYING DYLAN STRANGLED AGGIE!
THEY SAY THEY HAVE PROOF!
LISTEN TO ME. DYLAN COULDN'T HAVE KILLED AGGIE, RIGHT?
BECAUSE...
BECAUSE...
BECAUSE...HE'S HUMAN, AND A HUMAN CAN'T KILL A VAMPIRE. AGGIE WOULD'VE OVERPOWERED HIM IN A SECOND.
EXACTLY.
B-BUT THERE'S NO SUCH THINGS AS VAMPIRES...
DON'T WORRY, OLIVER ALREADY KNOWS.
I'M A CONDUIT. WE'LL EXPLAIN LATER.

JACK TOLD ME THERE'S SOMETHING OUT THERE KILLING BLUE BLOODS.

MY GUESS IS DYLAN IS BEING FRAMED.

BY WHO?

WE NEED TO FIND OUT WHY HE'S BEING CHARGED ALL OF A SUDDEN. WHERE DID THEY GET THIS "PROOF," WHEN THEY SAID SHE DIED OF AN OVERDOSE?

AND WHY PIN IT ON DYLAN?

MY DAD'S A SENATOR. MAYBE HE HAS SOME CONNECTIONS WITH THE POLICE.

GOOD. ASK HIM TO CHECK INTO IT.

SKY, I NEVER THOUGHT I'D SAY THIS, BUT YOU NEED TO TALK TO JACK.

PART IV: SHOTS IN THE DARK

DID YOU HEAR ABOUT DYLAN? WE HAVE TO *DO SOMETHING.*

IT'S NONE OF OUR BUSINESS.

WHAT?

DON'T YOU--DIDN'T YOU WANT TO--

I MADE A MISTAKE.

THE COMMITTEE INVESTIGATED AGGIE'S DEATH, AND WE NEED TO TRUST THEM TO DO WHAT'S BEST.

WHAT'S GOTTEN INTO YOU?

THE THINGS YOU TOLD ME... WHAT YOU SAID ABOUT *US*...

THAT WAS A MISTAKE, TOO. IT'S NOT THE WAY I FEEL.

I'M SORRY TO HAVE MISLED YOU.

BUT...

ALL MY DAD WOULD SAY IS THAT DYLAN IS BEING TAKEN CARE OF. HE TOLD ME TO STAY OUT OF IT.

WHAT ABOUT JACK? CAN HE HELP?

NO...

THEN IT'S UP TO US.

OH, MASTER RENFIELD...

YOUNG HAZARD-PERRY. ACTING THE *TRUANT*, I WAGER.

UM...WE'RE HERE FOR A CLASS PROJECT.

WE'RE RESEARCHING SOMETHING CALLED "CROATAN." EVER HEARD OF IT?

CROATAN. I SEE...

IT'S NOT A TERM I'M FAMILIAR WITH.

BEST OF LUCK WITH YOUR "CLASS PROJECT."

WE'VE BEEN AT THIS FOR HOURS. SO MANY BOOKS--

--SO LITTLE TIME.

IF IT'S EVER HAPPENED TO A VAMPIRE, THOUGH, IT'S IN THIS LIBRARY SOMEWHERE.

≥sigh≤

GUYS!

LOOK WHAT I FOUND.

LET'S TAKE THIS AROUND THE CORNER.

SKY, YOU SAID JACK MENTIONED THAT HE THOUGHT CROATAN HAD SOMETHING TO DO WITH PLYMOUTH COLONY, RIGHT?

YEAH.

WELL, THERE'S A SHELF IN THE HISTORY SECTION WITH BOOKS ABOUT WHEN THE BLUE BLOODS SETTLED MASSACHUSETTS.

I FOUND THIS DIARY FROM A *MAYFLOWER* WOMAN NAMED CATHERINE CARVER.

LOOK HERE.

Nothing remains of Roanoke except a bare patch of field. That, and a tree carved with a single, terrible word: Croatan. We are cursed! The enemy is here.

WHOA...

WHAT DO YOU THINK IT MEANS?

THERE DOESN'T SEEM TO BE ANY OTHER MENTION OF THE WORD.

IT SOUNDS LIKE WHOEVER CATHERINE CARVER WAS, SHE BELIEVED ROANOKE WAS FOUNDED BY BLUE BLOODS, TOO, AND THAT CROATAN WIPED THEM OUT.

IT'S LIKE THE REST OF THE PAGES HAVE BEEN TORN OUT OR SOMETHING...

WHY WOULD SOMEBODY DO THAT?

GOOD QUESTION.

SEE IF THERE'S A LIST OF PEOPLE WHO'VE CHECKED OUT THE BOOK. MAYBE WE CAN ASK ONE OF THEM.

WELL?

ENJOY YOUR DINNER, MADAM?

THE PRIME RIB WAS *OVERCOOKED*.

GRANDDAUGHTER. I AM SURPRISED TO SEE YOU.

LET'S RETURN SCHUYLER HOME, JULIUS.

YES, MADAM.

WHIRRR

SO YOU'VE FOUND CATHERINE'S DIARY.

I LEFT MY NAME IN IT FOR SOMEONE TO FIND, BUT I HARDLY EXPECTED IT WOULD BE YOU.

WHAT'S *CROATAN?*

IT'S AN ANCIENT WORD THAT MEANS *"SILVER BLOOD."*

WHAT I AM ABOUT TO TELL YOU IS *VERBOTEN.* THE COMMITTEE HAS LEGISLATED IT OUT OF EXISTENCE. THEY HAVE EVEN TRIED TO *SUPPRESS* IT FROM OUR MEMORIES.

IF ASKED TODAY, THE WOMAN WHO WROTE THAT DIARY WOULD DISOWN HER WORDS.

HOW DO *YOU* KNOW?

BECAUSE IT'S MY DIARY, OF COURSE. I AM CATHERINE CARVER.

I'D HOPED TO RECORD THE JOYOUS ARRIVAL OF OUR KIND IN THE NEW WORLD. LITTLE DID I KNOW HOW *TERRIBLE* THAT FIRST WINTER WOULD BE...

WHY? WHAT HAPPENED?

"EARLY IN OUR HISTORY--NOT LONG AFTER WE WERE EXPELLED FROM PARADISE-- *LUCIFER* AND A SMALL GROUP OF HIS LOYAL FOLLOWERS BROKE OFF FROM OUR GROUP.

"THEY WERE CONTEMPTUOUS OF OUR EXPULSION AND DID NOT WANT TO REGAIN THE LORD'S GRACE. THEY *REJECTED* THE CODE OF THE VAMPIRES."

THEY DISCOVERED THAT FEEDING ON OTHER VAMPIRES--CONSUMING BLUE BLOODS TO *COMPLETE DISSIPATION*--INCREASED THEIR POWER.

IT ALLOWED THEM TO ACQUIRE THEIR VICTIMS' ABILITIES, THEIR LIFE FORCE... EVEN THEIR *MEMORIES.*

"BUT IT CAME WITH A PRICE...

"THEIR BLOOD TURNED SILVER, AND THEY BECAME CROATAN. ABOMINATIONS, *INSANE* WITH THE LIVES OF THE MANY VAMPIRES IN THEIR HEADS."

YOU MEAN THEIR VICTIMS ARE STILL...ALIVE?

IN A SENSE, YES. FORCED TO LIVE AN *ETERNITY OF TORMENT* IN THE MIND OF THEIR MURDERER.

THE LAST GREAT WAR AGAINST THE CROATAN WAS DURING THE TIME OF THE ROMAN EMPIRE, WHEN WE WERE ABLE TO UNSEAT THE POWERFUL AND WILY SILVER BLOOD *CALIGULA.*

FOR CENTURIES WE THOUGHT THE THREAT WAS EXTINGUISHED...UNTIL ROANOKE WAS RAVAGED, AND OUR OWN CHILDREN BEGAN TO DISAPPEAR.

BLUE BLOODS ARE MOST VULNERABLE DURING ADOLESCENCE, WHEN WE TRANSFORM FROM HUMAN TO VAMPIRE.

NOT YET IN COMMAND OF OUR MEMORIES, WE ARE WEAK AND CAN BE MANIPULATED.

THIS IS A *DANGEROUS TIME* FOR YOU, CHILD.

WHY WON'T ANYONE PUT A STOP TO IT? WE HAVE TO *FIGHT* THEM!

IT HAS BEEN TOO LONG SINCE THE LAST ATTACK. WE HAVE GROWN COMPLACENT, RELUCTANT TO CONSIDER THAT ANYTHING COULD CHALLENGE OUR POWER.

AND OUR LEADER, CHARLES FORCE--*MYLES STANDISH*, AS HE WAS ONCE KNOWN-- HAS NEVER BELIEVED THAT THE CROATAN COULD RETURN...

BUT I FEAR A POTENT SILVER BLOOD HAS DONE JUST THAT, AND IS GATHERING *NEW DISCIPLES.*

THEY COULD BE ANYONE. SILVER BLOODS DISGUISED AS BLUE BLOODS IN OUR MIDST. THEY MIGHT NOT EVEN BE AWARE OF THEIR TRUE NATURE.

THAT HAS TO BE WHAT KILLED AGGIE! THEY'VE ARRESTED MY FRIEND, BUT HE *COULDN'T* HAVE DONE IT.

WE HAVE TO TELL EVERYONE. WE'LL *MAKE* THEM BELIEVE!

I HAVE TRIED BEFORE TO SOUND THE ALARM. I HAVE URGED ETERNAL VIGILANCE. I WAS *BANISHED* BECAUSE OF MY EFFORTS.

I HAVE TOLD YOU THE TRUTH. I CAN DO NO MORE.

THAT'S IT? YOU REALLY AREN'T GOING TO HELP?

CHARLES FORCE IS THE ONLY ONE WHO CAN HELP YOU NOW.

GOOD NIGHT.

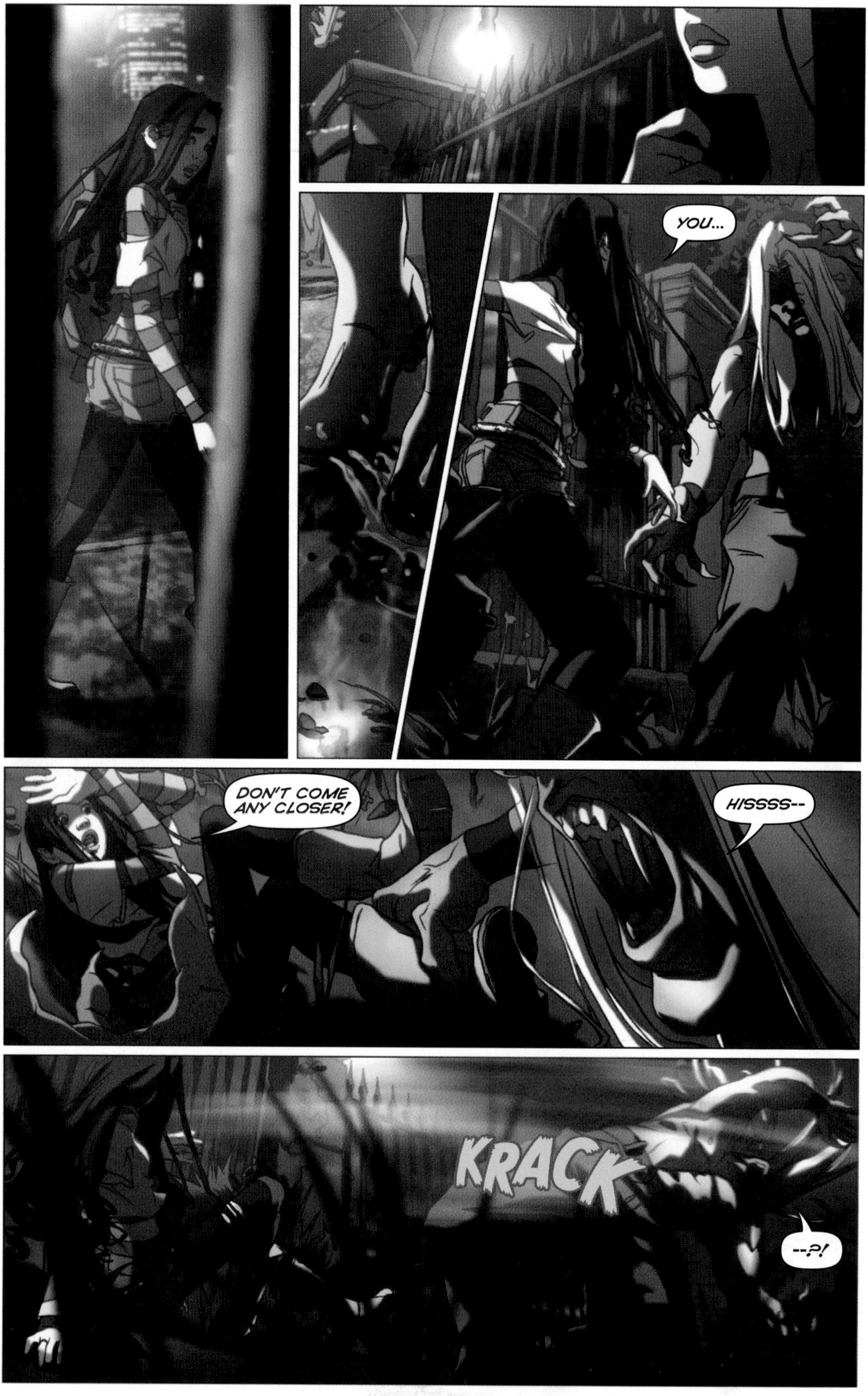
YOU...
DON'T COME ANY CLOSER!
HISSSS--
KRACK
--?!

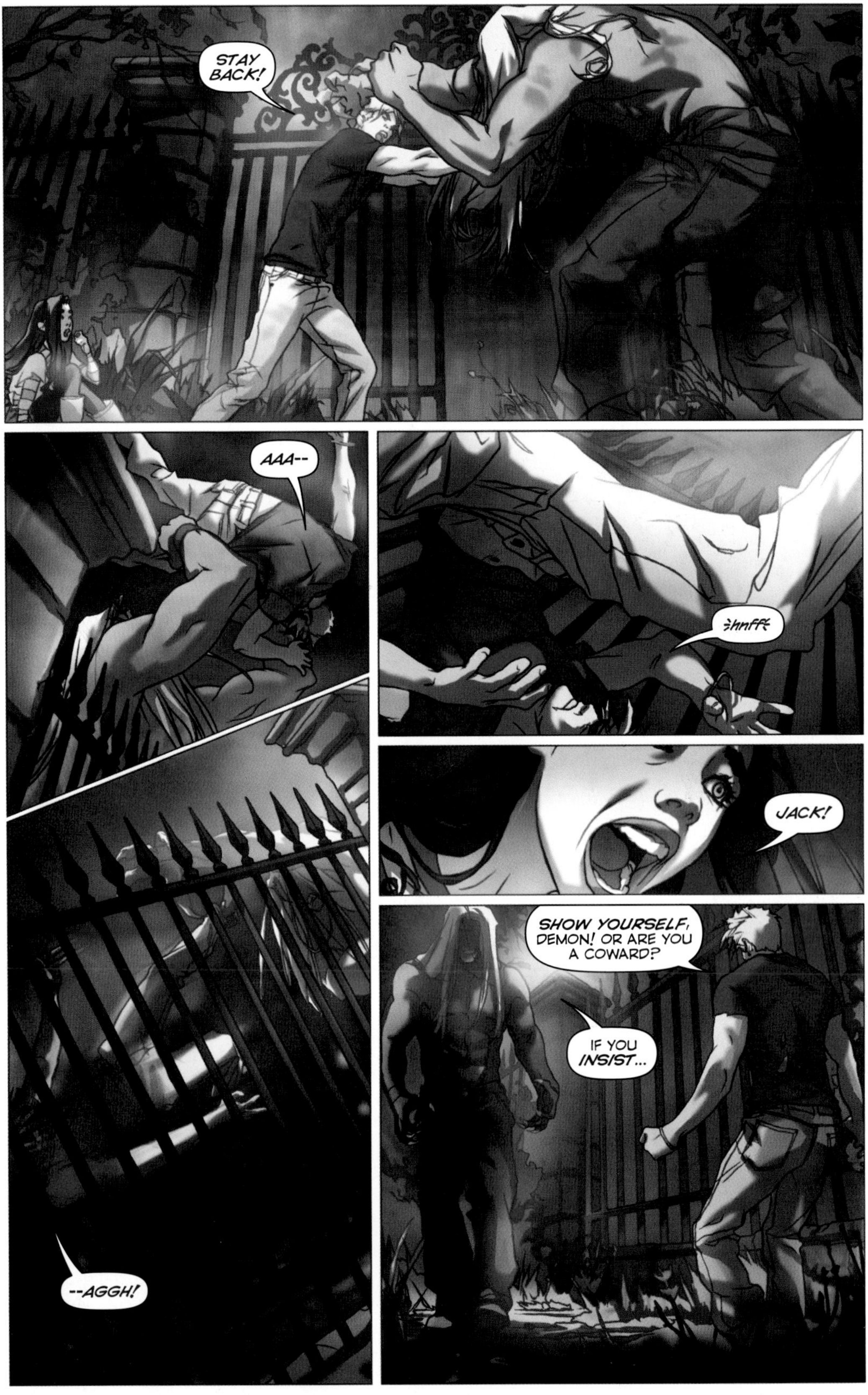
STAY BACK!
AAA--
⩥hnff⩤
--AGGH!
JACK!
SHOW YOURSELF, DEMON! OR ARE YOU A COWARD?
IF YOU INSIST...

NO...IT'S NOT POSSIBLE...

HAHAHA

HIS FACE...

IT HAS TO BE A MISTAKE. A TRICK OF THE LIGHT OR SOMETHING.

I SAW IT, TOO. THERE'S NO MISTAKE.

I'M SORRY...

JACK, HE MIGHT NOT EVEN KNOW WHAT HE IS. WE HAVE TO FIND HIM.

I JUST SAW HIM AT DINNER...

HE SAID HE WAS GOING TO SEE SOMEONE AT THE HOSPITAL.

FSSHT

FSSHT

GET AWAY FROM HER!

LOWER YOUR VOICE, AND SHOW SOME RESPECT FOR YOUR SURROUNDINGS.

YOU'RE IN A HOSPITAL, NOT AT A WRESTLING MATCH.

CROATAN!

WHAT EXACTLY ARE YOU ACCUSING ME OF?

YOU ATTACKED SCHUYLER.

I SAW THE BEAST'S FACE, AND IT WAS *YOURS*.

TIMES HAVE CERTAINLY CHANGED IF *MY OWN SON* THINKS I AM ABOMINATION.

THE ACCUSATION WOULD BE INSULTING IF IT WASN'T SO *ABSURD*.

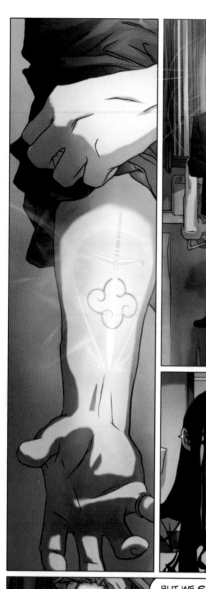

FORGIVE ME, FATHER. I HAVE BEEN LOST, BUT NOW I AM FOUND.

RISE, MY SON. THERE IS NOTHING TO FORGIVE.

WHAT'S GOING ON? WHAT DOES THAT SYMBOL MEAN?

IT'S THE *MARK OF THE ARCHANGEL*. IT CAN'T BE DUPLICATED OR FALSIFIED.

IT MEANS MY FATHER IS MICHAEL, PURE OF HEART, WHO VOLUNTARILY ACCOMPANIED THE BANISHED TO EARTH TO GUIDE US IN OUR JOURNEY.

BUT WE *SAW* THE MONSTER'S FACE!

WHAT YOU SAW WAS NO DOUBT THE *RUSE* OF AN AGILE SHAPE-SHIFTER WHO HOPED TO TURN MY SON AGAINST ME.

TO WHAT END, I DO NOT KNOW.

IF YOU DIDN'T KILL AGGIE, THEN *WHO DID*?

AND WHERE'S DYLAN?

WE HAD HIM UNDER LOCK AND KEY, BUT HE WAS ABLE TO FREE HIMSELF. IT SEEMS HIS ABILITIES ARE MORE DEVELOPED THAN WE HAD GUESSED.

ABILITIES?

DYLAN IS A BLUE BLOOD. I THOUGHT YOU KNEW.

HE'S A VAMPIRE? THEN THAT MEANS...

OH, GOD... IF HE'S REALLY A SILVER BLOOD, WE HAVE TO WARN BLISS!

JUST LIKE YOUR GRANDMOTHER, YOU ARE. PRONE TO HYSTERIA. I'VE SAID IT BEFORE, AND I'LL SAY IT AGAIN: THERE ARE NO SILVER BLOODS.

I WAS AT THE BATTLE OF ROME, CHILD. I SENT LUCIFER HIMSELF TO THE FIRES OF HELL.

IT'S FAR MORE PLAUSIBLE THAT YOUR FRIEND MERELY SUFFERS FROM DEMENTIA. TRANSITION IS A VOLATILE TIME FOR OUR KIND, AND NOT EVERYONE HANDLES THE CHANGE PEACEFULLY.

NOW, RETURN HOME, BOTH OF YOU. THERE IS STILL A CHANCE TO SAVE MR. WARD'S IMMORTAL SOUL.

THAT IS WHY I CAME HERE TO ENSURE YOUR MOTHER'S SAFETY... SHE IS IN NO CONDITION TO DEFEND HERSELF.

"BUT FIRST--"

"--HE MUST BE FOUND."

>gasp<

BLISS...

SOMETHING'S HAPPENING TO ME... I THINK I TRIED TO KILL SCHUYLER.

NO. NO WAY. YOU *COULDN'T* HAVE!

YOU DON'T UNDERSTAND. I'M LIKE YOU.

I'M A *VAMPIRE.*

I THINK I KILLED AGGIE, TOO.

I'M SO SORRY...

NO... PLEASE...

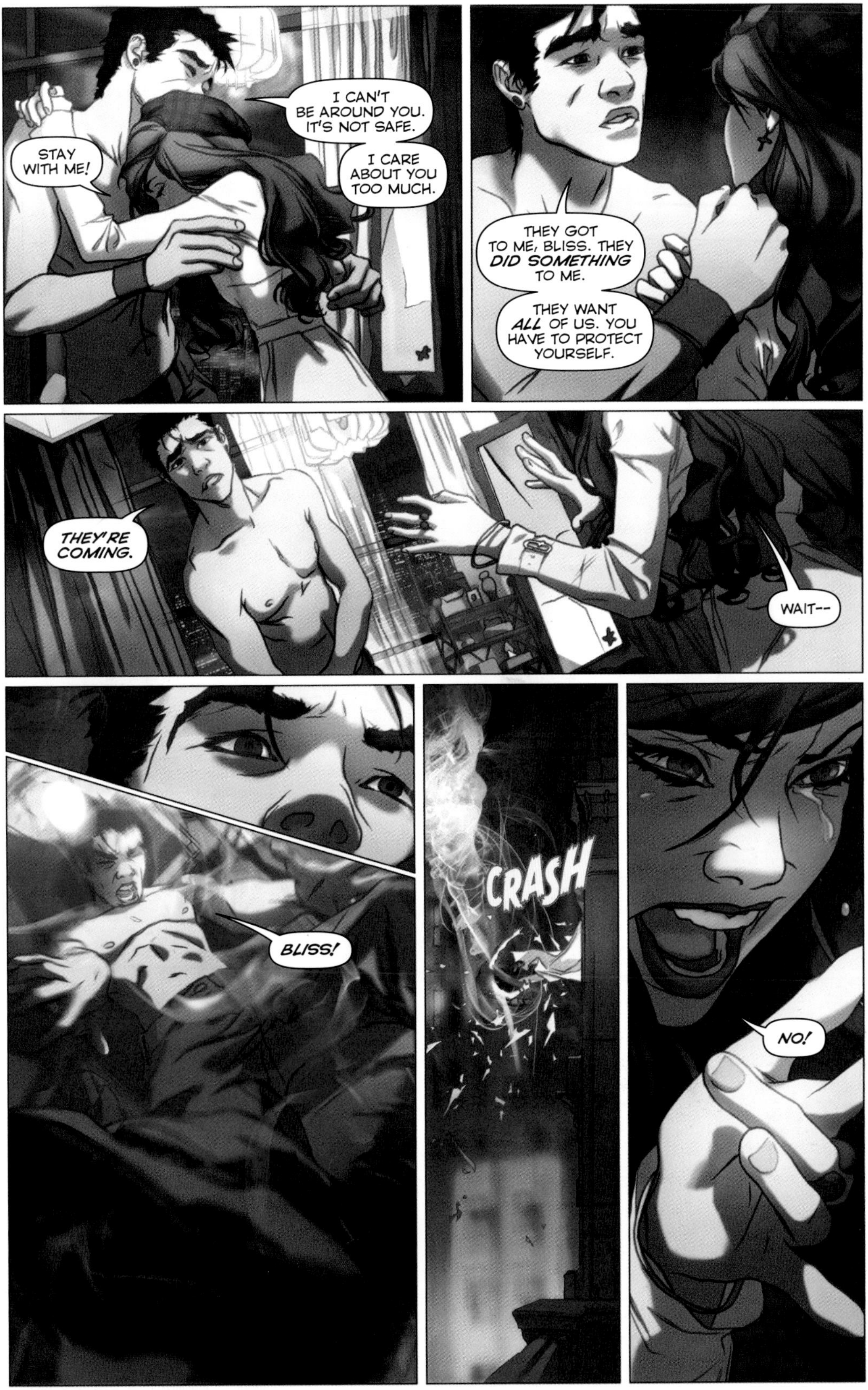
STAY WITH ME!
I CAN'T BE AROUND YOU. IT'S NOT SAFE.
I CARE ABOUT YOU TOO MUCH.
THEY GOT TO ME, BLISS. THEY DID SOMETHING TO ME.
THEY WANT ALL OF US. YOU HAVE TO PROTECT YOURSELF.
THEY'RE COMING.
WAIT--
BLISS!
CRASH
NO!

NO!

$pant$
$pant$

ARE YOU OKAY...? I HEARD NOISES.

I'M *FINE*, JORDAN.

JUST A... BAD DREAM IS ALL.

NO, IT WASN'T.

LOOK.

CORDELIA! WE NEED TO TALK!

CORDELIA?

uhnnnn...

CORDELIA!

CROATAN...

FOUGHT IT OFF...BUT SO STRONG...

THIS CYCLE IS ENDED FOR ME. ≈cough≈

THIS IS THE LAST WE WILL SPEAK FOR A LONG TIME.

NO...

LISTEN, CHILD.
THERE IS MUCH YOU
NEED TO KNOW.

YOUR MOTHER'S
TRUE NAME IS GABRIELLE.
SHE IS AN ARCHANGEL...ONE
OF OUR STRONGEST.

SHE DOES NOT
WAKE UP BECAUSE SHE
REFUSES TO TAKE THE
RED BLOOD TO KEEP
HER ALIVE.

WHEN YOUR
FATHER DIED, SHE SWORE
TO PRESERVE THEIR LOVE BY
NEVER TAKING ANOTHER
HUMAN FAMILIAR.

ANOTHER...

MY FATHER
WAS *HUMAN?*

YES. YOU ARE
*DIMIDIUM
COGNATUS.*
A *HALF BLOOD.*

YOU ARE
THE ONLY ONE...
AND IT IS SAID
THAT THE DAUGHTER
OF GABRIELLE
WILL LEAD US TO
SALVATION.

ME?
HOW?

FIND
YOUR GRANDFATHER.
HE IS AN *ENMORTAL...*
A VAMPIRE WHO HAS
KEPT THE SAME
PHYSICAL SHELL FOR
CENTURIES.

AFTER WE
WERE BANISHED,
WE SEPARATED...
BUT YOU MUST FIND
HIM NOW. ONLY HE
KNOWS HOW TO
DEFEAT THE SILVER
BLOODS.

GO TO
VENICE. HE WAS
ALWAYS FOND
OF ITALY...

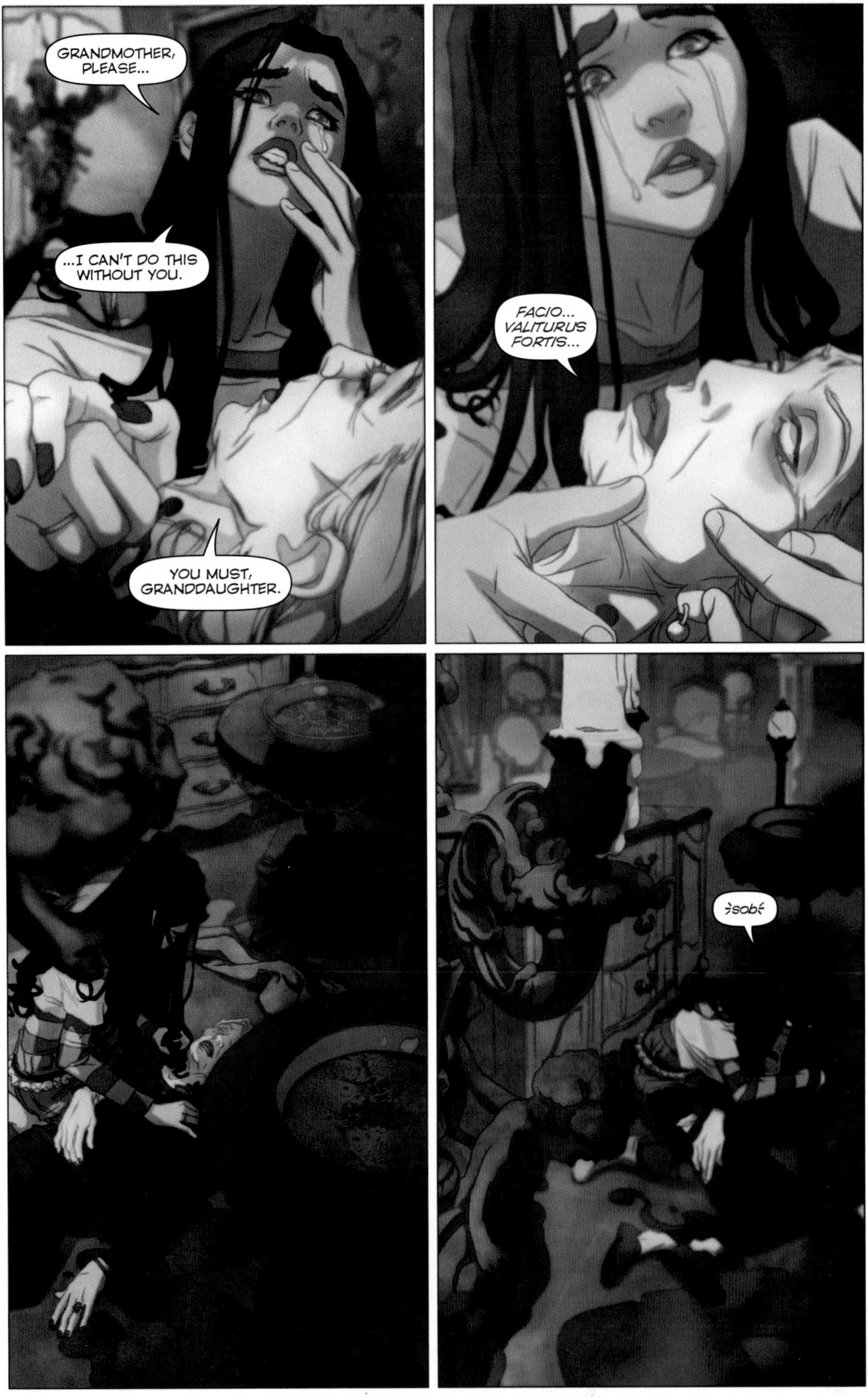
GRANDMOTHER, PLEASE...
...I CAN'T DO THIS WITHOUT YOU.
YOU MUST, GRANDDAUGHTER.
FACIO... VALITURUS FORTIS...
sob

CORDELIA VAN ALEN
VOS VADUM REVERTO

SCHUYLER, CAN I TALK TO YOU FOR A SEC?

WHAT WOULD YOU LIKE TO SAY?

JUST THAT I'M SORRY THINGS WENT SO WEIRD BETWEEN US...

I...MY LIFE ISN'T MY OWN. I HAVE RESPONSIBILITIES TO MY FAMILY THAT PRECLUDE THE KIND OF... RELATIONSHIP WE--

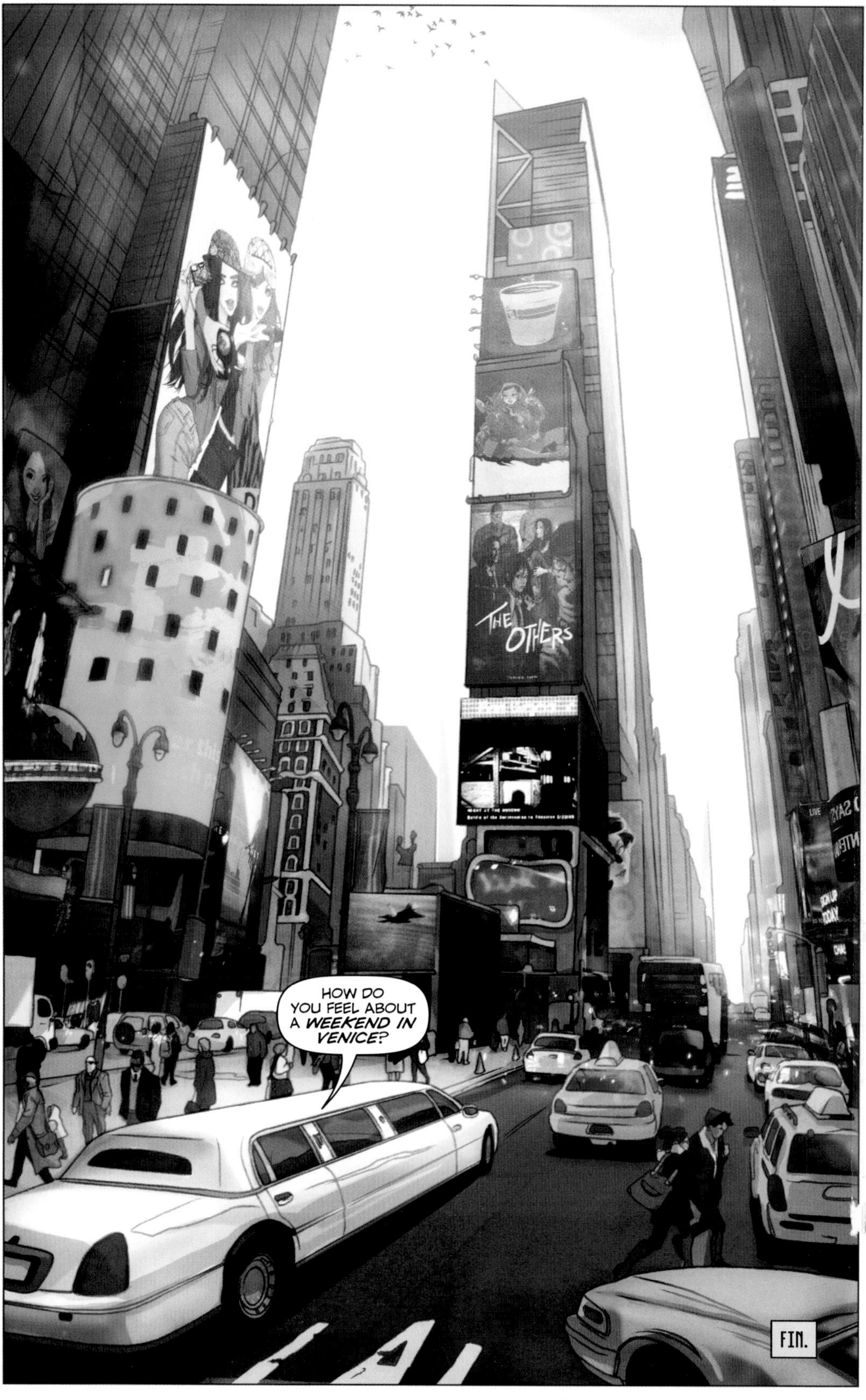
THE OTHERS
HOW DO YOU FEEL ABOUT A *WEEKEND IN VENICE*?
FIN.

YOU DON'T HAVE TO EXPLAIN.

YOU NEED TO DO WHAT *YOU* NEED TO DO, AND I NEED TO DO WHAT *I* NEED TO DO.

SCHUYLER, I...

SKY? THE CAR IS WAITING.

GOOD-BYE, JACK.

YOU HEAR ABOUT THE PREPPIE KID THEY FOUND DEAD AT A PARTY?

LANDON SCHLESSINGER. HE WAS AT THE COMMITTEE MEETINGS.

SOMEHOW, I DON'T THINK IT WAS AN *OVERDOSE* THAT DID HIM IN, EITHER.

WHAT ARE WE GOING TO DO ABOUT IT?

THAT DEPENDS...